D1255759

Mollie Make-Believe

Mollie Make-Believe

————————— *by Alice Bach*

Harper & Row, Publishers
New York   Evanston   San Francisco   London

35,592

LIBRARY OF CONGRESS CATALOG CARD NUMBER: 73–14334
TRADE STANDARD BOOK NUMBER: 06–020315–3
HARPERCREST STANDARD BOOK NUMBER: 06–020316–1

FIRST EDITION

Mollie Make-Believe

Chapter One

At about ten o'clock on a Saturday morning in late June, Mollie Fields was sitting at the top of the stairs looking down at her father. John Fields was kneeling in front of the guts of a stereo receiver spread out in a semicircle around him. He was wearing a faded pink-and-gray-plaid cotton shirt, the cuffs drawn back past his elbows, shapeless khaki trousers, and a pair of soft-soled Indian moccasins with most of the beadwork gone. How different from his narrow ties, dark suits, and wing-tipped weekday shoes. Father seemed covered with layers of cloth when he went to the office, an impersonal man. It was only on Saturdays when Mollie could watch him that whatever small communication there was between them took place.

"What's wrong with it, Dad?"

"There's some noise in the bass." He didn't turn around to answer his daughter. "Hand me the screwdriver, will you?"

1

"Sure." Mollie jammed her feet into the sandals on the step below her and adjusted the straps as she went down the stairs. She rummaged through his toolbox until she found a yellow plastic-handled screwdriver. "God, Dad, how long have you had this one? I used to hand it to you when I was a little kid."

"If you take care of things, you'll have them a long time."

"Hey, Dad. . . ."

"Don't 'hey' me, Mollie," he said, concentrating on the transformer.

"Sorry. Do you remember how I used to watch you every Saturday? Stand around looking while you wired stuff down in the lab."

"Naturally I remember. Hold that wire like so." She picked it up from him, trying to copy the way he was holding the wire.

"Not that way, this way." His fingers moved deftly among the coils and circuits of the receiver.

"Are you in a bad mood?" Mollie had a special decoding ear for her family. She listened not to their words, but to their tone of voice.

"Certainly not. Pull the wire toward you just a bit while I solder this end."

Mayhew, Mollie's brother, never became involved with Father this way. Mayhew had a habit of disappearing after breakfast and reappearing somewhere between the time Mother sighed, "Where is your brother?" and dinner.

"OK, Mollie, you can let go now."

She wondered why he took something apart every weekend, to improve it, refine it, fix it, alter it. She went into the kitchen, poured some coffee, and returned to the stairs.

2

"What are you going to do today?" Father asked.

"Why does everyone have to have a project?"

"I don't want you lounging around all summer. Why don't you clean the garage or organize some of those cartons in the attic?"

"Cripes, Dad. I don't need a project."

"You're old enough to pull your own weight, Mollie."

"Suppose I change my name to Mollieangelo and paint the living-room ceiling."

"Don't be wise." Father's voice had lost its automatic quality. He was listening now. If she didn't move fast, she'd end up cleaning the garage.

"Yes, sir." She took her coffee cup back to the kitchen. This was going to be a long summer, and they would definitely not allow her to "lounge around" as her father had put it. In a couple of months, I'll be away at school and they won't be able to tell me what to do anymore. But it's a long time till then, she thought. If only I could please them. Her father walked into the kitchen. "Dad, I'll do the garage next week, OK?" He nodded and she went upstairs trying to figure out some project for the day that would not be too revolting.

"Mother, can I cook the whole dinner tonight?"

"No, dear. I have the menu all planned." Mother was seated at her dressing table studying her eyes in a magnifying mirror, all her equipment in a gold-flecked, partitioned plastic tray next to her.

"Can I bake a pie or a cake?"

"Your father told me last night he doesn't want any more desserts. Mollie, I told you this would happen. You must have structure to your days. You can't just wander around the house every day." Mother bent closer to her reflection, her

3

outline framed by the theatrical lights that surrounded her mirror.

"Then I'll bake a pie."

"Mollie, we are not going to go through this all summer." Her mother smoothed her left eyebrow and reached for a mascara brush.

"Go through what?"

"Mollie—"

Mother took a huge breath, and Mollie left the room calling over her shoulder, "You already did that eye." How can anyone spend so long staring into a mirror, she thought. I couldn't load up my face with all that crap, no matter what. Mollie picked up the telephone and dialed, saying each number softly under her breath. As she waited for an answer, she said dramatically, "The evidence grows stronger with each passing day that I must be a changeling."

"Hi, Hil. It's me. What's up?"

"Nothing. It's Saturday, remember?" Hilary's parents insisted she work around the house on Saturday. She had her own car and more clothes than anybody at school, but the working on Saturday made her parents feel better.

"Think you'll be done early?"

"Ha. You ask me the same thing every Saturday." They both laughed. Mollie was annoyed that she and Hilary, her best friend, could never do anything together on Saturdays because of Hilary's work rule.

"Well, some week they may change their minds."

"Not likely. Listen, I'd better get moving. I haven't even had breakfast yet. I'll call you later."

I should have made plans with David, or somebody, Mollie thought.

4

The telephone rang. Maybe Hilary had gotten out of Saturday work. Maybe David wanted to come over.

"Good morning," she said cheerfully.

"Morning, Mollie. Let me speak with your father, please."

"Reed, good morning. How are you? And Grandmother? Are you coming out this weekend?" Her grandfather was the person Mollie loved most in the world. Her decoding ear found pride and happiness in Reed's voice when he talked with her. He had been nicknamed Reed, "the hardiest of the Fieldses," half a century ago while he was still at college. At seventy, he was a vigorous man, with heavy white hair slashed with ivory streaks. Tall, lean, and—some said—vain.

"Not today. Let me talk to Dad." He sounded grim, so Mollie hurried to get her father.

Reed had married Grandmother early in the century. Even now they held hands under the table, sought each other's eye across the room. Flora was small and full of energy. She had ropes of hair wound round her head, dark glittering eyes, and tiny dimpled hands. She was not a lap-sitting grandmother. She was tough and hard; there were no crevices for a little girl to curl up inside. Grandmother was as perfectly polished as her oval dark-red nails. And Grandmother's opinion was the final judgment on anything for Mollie.

When Mollie had been eight, she had decided to call Grandmother GM.

"Mollie, my name is Grandmother. Don't try to embellish it or improve it. Just call me Grandmother. It's bad enough that your brother is called Hew. What is this family's passion for corrupting given names?"

5

Mollie had looked at Grandmother, anxious to please her, yet unsure about her reaction. "Mayhew keeps getting teased on the playground."

Grandmother had stared at Mollie. "Whatever for?" she said.

"I think because his name is Mayhew."

"Wherever do you get such ideas? Mayhew was my maiden name." The tone in her voice ended the discussion.

Reed wasn't like Grandmother. And he certainly wasn't like her parents. He had always liked Mollie. He had always believed whatever she told him and seemed to understand just what she was saying—when she was being funny, he laughed; when she was being serious, he nodded and listened. Mollie felt he understood her, and he did not judge her as harshly as the rest of the family did.

"Mollie, your grandmother appears to be ill. Mother and I are going into the city to visit her. You'll have to supervise Mayhew." Father's face showed no expression. "We'll call you from the city to make sure everything is under control here." He shouted up the stairs. "Cynthia, hurry up. I told Dad we were leaving right away."

"Mollie, there's hamburger in the freezer. You'd better defrost it now, and in the blue bowl is some leftover spinach. . . ." Mother was clutching a fistful of jewelry as she hurried down the stairs.

"C'mon, Cyn, surely Mollie can fix dinner for the two of them." Her father's impatience made Mollie stiffen.

"Be responsible, Mollie. Don't fight with Hew and don't either of you wander off anywhere," she said, head bent to fasten a strand of pearls, the clasp tangling in the short hairs on the back of her neck.

6

"Hew's already left."

"Mollie, try to cooperate."

"It's not my fault . . ."

"Find your brother, dear; then both of you stay put."
Two twisted gold rope bracelets, and gold shell earrings.
One last look in the mirror. It's a good thing we have them
all over the house. Mollie narrowed her eyes as she watched
her mother smooth a stray hair.

"And don't forget to clean up the kitchen, dear." Mother
kissed her and drifted out the door in an aura of Arpege.
Mollie turned away from the sticky-sweet smell. She kicked
off her shoes and watched the long blue car glide down the
driveway, soundless as a great fish. They were finally gone.

The whole day belonged to Mollie! She opened the
refrigerator and reached for a jar of blackberry jam. She
dipped a finger into the center of the dark shiny jam and
sucked it off her finger. She held the refrigerator door open
with her other hand. The chill air swirled around her. She
uncapped the milk bottle, took a long cold swallow, and
grinned. How wonderful to be alone, unobserved all day.

She knew Grandmother wasn't really sick. A headache,
maybe.

A couple of slices of bologna, a sweet pickle, another
swig of milk. Maybe I'll watch rotten movies all day. No
projects, no good works.

She walked into the living room. If it were her room,
she'd get rid of that stiff beige couch. And those dark green
chairs with the frail fruitwood arms. She'd have plump
yellow chairs, and a green woolly rug that looked like real
grass. She moved a bowl of zinnias from the mantelpiece
to the coffee table. A beam of sunlight shone on them like

7

a spotlight, clearly defining each stubby petal and filling the space above the table with vivid purple.

Mollie stared at the flowers, wishing she could absorb some of their purple richness. These zinnias were special to her because they were purple; she disliked orange zinnias; they seemed garish and stiff. She was sure she would never have had any lasting joy from the thought of a yellow unicorn or have felt cozy under a harsh gray army blanket. She'd have to ask Mother if she could take her quilt to college.

College. Mollie got excited whenever the word went through her head. Springfield without any of the family. Springfield—starting fresh as a brand-new person. All the way through school, there had been her older cousin Holly, funny, pretty, attracting the most attractive boys. An impossible act to follow. Now, with Holly off at drama school, Mollie would be alone. The family had always been the walls off which Mollie had careened. Springfield would mean living without those walls.

"Hey, Moll, where are they?" Mayhew was standing in front of her, stretching the waist of a blue madras bathing suit in his hands. He was small for his age. He had dull straight hair and a timid hesitant look. He held his left shoulder slightly higher than his right, adding to his tentative appearance.

"They went into the city. Grandmother is sick."

"Very sick?"

"Of course not, stupid. I talked to her yesterday. They won't be back for dinner." Mollie smiled and said in a singsong voice, "And you have to obey me."

"Good luck. I'm going swimming with Porky."

"They said for both of us to stay here."

"Just pretend you didn't see me. I'll be back before they are anyway, so they'll never know."

"Unless I tell them." Mollie automatically teased Hew. They had fought all the time when they were younger. But they had been growing closer in the last couple of years, mutual grievances binding them together more than mutual pleasures. Mollie felt sorry for her brother. He would be alone, dealing with the family once she was off at Springfield. If things got rough, she could count on Reed, but Hew had nobody. She'd have to send him cartoons and funny letters from college.

"Go ahead. You know I won't say anything. Just be damn sure to be here by five. In case they come back early. I don't want any hassle because you're off swimming with Porky."

"I'll be back by four!" He ran out the door, leaving Mollie to the quiet of the house.

It was odd to see Mayhew running off enthusiastically, to go swimming. Neither of them was athletic. How she had been tricked by the archery range and the baseball field! Girls who had been friends moved away from you if you couldn't hit the bull's eye or hit a home run. And Mollie never could!

Those long summers at camp—those unending sweating mornings standing far away in right field. As the game progressed, Mollie would step back even farther, hoping that none of those screaming amazons could hit the ball that far. She could still hear the hollow thwack the bat made when it connected with the ball, whacking it into right field. Then all her teammates would scream, "Catch it!" "Throw it to me!" "Get it to second!" as Mollie squinted into the over-bright sky, waiting for the ball to come hurtling toward her. She never caught it, never came close to executing one of those balletlike leaps that put Willie Mays on the front page. One or two times she had at least grabbed at the ball as it bounced off the ground and tried to throw it—but the ball landed like lead, closer to Mollie than to her zealous teammate. She could feel the damnation as the girls glowered at her, even though she stared fixedly at the umpire, avoiding all their glances.

She had loved the late-night campfires. Sitting in the dark pine grove, her front side warmed by the fire and her back almost cold from the pine-soaked breeze. Toasting marshmallows on a special stick from the woods behind the cabin, with the toasting end sharpened to a point. Charred marshmallows with soft gluey white insides, sticking the corners of her lips together. Singing songs and looking across the circle as they swayed with arms around each other. Everybody's face looked kind in the firelight, not mean and threatening like on the sun-filled baseball field. Songs and soft smiles and then standing, singing "Taps" and looking up into the purple sky that started just above the pointed tops of swaying pines. But all that warmth could not fill Mollie; she could not save the quiet campfire inside her for the next morning on that August-dry field where the bright sun looked like a large baseball, waiting for Mollie, ready to elude her as the smaller version always did.

The first year had been the hardest. The two summers after that were not so bad. Most of the girls had accepted her by then, and the nicer counselors let her take extra arts and crafts instead of that hot, still time, standing so far from the real action of the game.

But what had it been like for Mayhew? It was worse for

boys who can't catch. Mollie had known about Mayhew since they had gone to the same school years earlier. She had seen her brother, about eight years old, standing alone on the playground. He was small, with ears that stuck out from his head like handles on a loving cup. He was standing quietly in his brown Windbreaker, squinting although it was a cloudy day. He wasn't even looking for someone to play with, wasn't even looking at the boys choosing up sides to play baseball. He just stood there.

Mollie felt sorry for him, but she was mad too. C'mon, Mayhew, she was screaming inside her head, find someone to play with. Don't stand there, out in the open, all alone. She quickly joined a group of chattering girls and moved into the center of their circle, to be warmed by their talk and to blot out the pain of seeing Mayhew's frailty.

Leaning against the couch and looking around her parents' living room, Mollie felt as though those days at camp had happened to some other girl. But every once in a while she would dream that she was searching a blindingly bright sky with silvery-white reflected all around. She was desperately searching for something, but she couldn't see anything in the overpowering brightness. She couldn't even keep her eyes open against the dazzling light. Then she'd wake up and shake the dream off and think: That's all over now. Nobody even thinks about baseball anymore.

Suddenly the house seemed oppressively still. Mollie turned on the radio; some disc jockey was screaming—more jarring than the silence. She snapped off the radio, went over to the telephone, and dialed Hilary again. She pictured Hilary running through the new wing of her long, spread-out house to get to the telephone.

Hilary would slump across the red lacquered chest that

11

held the telephone, a message pad, and one small lamp. Once Mollie had opened the chest and discovered old notebooks, outgrown sweaters, empty record jackets, an old Swiss Miss doll with her costume falling off, dried-out tubes of makeup—all shoved in, layer upon layer.

"Hilary, look at this crap. How can you tell where anything is?"

Hilary shrugged. "When I have to clean up in a hurry, I shove stuff in the chest. I could throw it all away cause I never take anything out of there. Just put more stuff in. But what's the difference? Nobody knows it's messy but me."

"Won't your parents have a stroke if they see it?"

"What the hell would they be doing in my chest?" They both giggled. Hilary said, "You know what I mean." I know what you mean, Mollie thought, but you don't know what I mean.

"Hilary, it's me again. My parents have gone to the city. They want me to hang around here and I'm so bored."

"How come you have to hang around?"

"They went in cause Reed called and said Grandmother is ill, which is crap. I talked to her yesterday and she was fine. Anyway, they'll be back after dinner. I have to feed Mayhew."

"Is she very sick, your grandmother?" Hilary never listened.

"Of course not. I just said I talked to her yesterday."

"Then why did they go rushing off into the city?"

Mollie switched the phone to her other ear. "Whenever Reed calls, they do that. He's like some old patriarch." They both snickered, but Mollie felt guilty. She felt safe and protected exactly because Reed ruled the family, and he would never let anything bad happen to her.

"Listen, good buddy, I gotta get to the rose garden. All the bushes have to be tied up. He's even supplied me with thick gloves that look like what linemen wear on the high wire. If I finish before dark, I'll come over. Unless he finds some more work. Bye."

What linemen wear. How would Hilary know? As Mollie thought about it, she had to admit she had no idea what linemen wore either. Damn. At least Hilary had something to do. Tie up those rose bushes. A job that she could finish today. Mollie thought of the attic. What a choice. Dusty attic or greasy garage. She wandered back into the kitchen and opened the refrigerator. Everything looked boring. Half-filled jars, and plastic containers. She slammed the door and went back up to her room.

Could Grandmother be really sick? She had seen her the other day. It's just because she's old. And you always think of old people getting sick with a capital S. Sick and then . . . But Grandmother old? She'd love to hear me call her old. She'd narrow her eyes, her hands perfectly still in her lap, and just stare. Then I'd start apologizing. Mollie could hold up in an argument with her parents, but a stare from Grandmother stopped her cold.

Grandmother with her beautiful dresses and coats lined to match. Grandmother with her glittering rings and snuggly fur coats. When Mollie had been little, she used to tuck her arm through Grandmother's and bury her face deep into the dense dark-brown fur. Until Grandmother would shake her off. "For God's sake, Mollie, don't *hang* on me. Walk properly." And Mollie would remove her arm and walk silently next to Grandmother, with Holly on Grandmother's other side.

She wondered if Grandmother ever guessed that when she came to visit and her coat was thrown across Mother's bed, Mollie would sneak upstairs and lie on the fur, rubbing her face in its softness and watching the sunlight change patches of fur from dark brown to caramel color. She'd lie there, smelling Grandmother's perfume which clung to all Grandmother's clothes, a stronger identification than a name tape. Like Cinderella's slipper, Grandmother's clothes could be worn by no one else. Mollie would lie on the fur and play with Grandmother's silk scarf. Oh what scarves Grandmother had. Such beautiful colors and so soft. Slippery soft, not warm soft like the fur. Mollie had thought about stealing one of Grandmother's scarves. She could keep it in her drawer and all her clothes would smell like Grandmother. But she knew that vague scent would lead them right to her. It was Grandmother's scarf and Mollie could only hold it, look at the sun through it, and fold it into a pillow as she lay on the fur coat up there on Mother's bed—and not for too long.

When Grandmother and Reed came to visit, she was expected downstairs, until it was time for her and Mayhew to have their supper. A hastily thrown-together sandwich in the kitchen, where they watched the grander preparations for the grown-ups' dinner later on. All Mollie and Mayhew would know of that would be the sound of muffled voices and sudden laughter drifting upstairs from the dining room, and the cold roast for lunch the next day.

Mollie dwindled away the day, poking in her desk drawers, resolving to throw away most of the bits and scraps of paper: tickets from school dances, menus from camp banquets, Christmas cards from favorite teachers, and two half-started diaries. In the end she put them all back in the drawer. Even when she was away at college, living a completely new life and storing up completely new names and events, here at home in her desk would be the details of her past.

"Mollie, Mollie, Mollie!" Mayhew's shouts broke through the peace of the house.

"You know where I am. Don't stand down there shouting. Come up here if you want to talk to me."

"Yes, Mother." Mayhew appeared in her doorway, hair slicked down, his arm wrapped around a damp loaflike towel, holding his wet bathing suit. "We had a great time. Porky pushed me in about fifty times."

"Sounds great."

"Wanna order a pizza for dinner? I have some money. We can throw away whatever they left for us. They'll never know."

"Hamburger and creamed spinach."

"That spinach we had last night?"

"The very same. There's some left."

"No wonder. It tasted like boiled shoelaces."

"That's the escarole." Mollie giggled in spite of herself. It had tasted like boiled shoelaces.

"Let's feed it to the disposal."

"No, we have to eat it, and the hamburger too." Mollie stopped. She had forgotten to take the meat out of the freezer. Mayhew took her hesitation for acquiesence.

"I'll call now and tell them five-thirty. Just sausage, or everything?"

"Mayhew, if we get caught—"

"I know; it was my idea."

"We can eat outside, away from the house so Mother

15

won't smell the oregano and garlic." She looked at her brother, measuring his trustworthiness. "Would you dig a hole out in back, past the willows'"

"What for? The pizza box?"

"No, some frozen hamburger." They both laughed loudly. It's nice for us to be able to share something, Mollie thought. It's been a long time since we laughed at the same thing.

"Hey, Moll, we can stick the pizza box in Mrs. Whitney's garbage."

"Terrific idea. And we'll take Cokes out to the willows. Tell them to put on extra sausage and extra cheese."

"Super. Let's have some ice cream before we bury the meat." Then, arms around each other, they went to the garage to get a shovel.

Chapter Two

Mollie loved to sleep late, to leave the soft world of blurred dreams slowly, to reconnect quietly with her room, radiant in midmorning sunshine. When she woke up too suddenly, not enough dreams to coat her mind, Mollie burrowed deeper into the center of the bed. She pulled her flower-print quilt up under her ears and poked her nose into a small cold valley in her pillow.

Today Mollie had been awake for a long time. Grandmother was still sick. Mollie couldn't picture Grandmother lying in bed. She had never seen her in a nightgown. A peignoir, yes. When she was little, Mollie would sit at the foot of the brocade chaise longue and watch Grandmother comb her hair. It billowed out around her, falling over her shoulders, down her back, almost to her waist. Sometimes Mollie would touch the ends of Grandmother's hair, letting the few strands dancing freely in a beam of sunlight brush against her fingers.

Once she began the twisting and braiding and controlling of the hair, Grandmother worked quickly. In a minute the mass of floating hair became an orderly tight braid wrapped around her head, in place for the day.

Grandmother had been fighting Mollie's hair for years. "You must learn to do your hair," she would say. Grandmother grasped Mollie's chin in one hand and combed her light-brown curly hair with the other. When the comb hit a tangle, Mollie's head would jerk, and Grandmother had to comb that much harder. Then she led Mollie by the chin into the bathroom and slicked her hair down with water. It's going to flap around as soon as it dries, Mollie always thought. But Grandmother repeated the ritual each time.

Holly had smooth hair, always combed, always flat. Mollie was bleached-out beside her cousin, whose rosy cheeks and shiny dark hair and eyes seemed to please Grandmother. Holly was the only grandchild she would call by a nickname. Hollister had been Aunt Pat's maiden name, and as the oldest girl in the family, Holly should have been named for Grandmother. But Grandmother didn't mind, even though names were important in the family. Mollie believed one reason Reed was so patient with her was that she was named for his mother. It was a distinction she was grateful for.

I wonder what kind of hair Reed had, Mollie thought. Was it flat and shiny like Grandmother's and Holly's? The few remaining photographs of Reed with young hair were too yellowed to tell. Once Mollie had asked him about his hair. "I had beautiful hair," he said. "People used to come from miles around just to see it."

"No, really, Reed, what was your hair like?" Mollie remembered how intent she was on the question. But she never found out. I wonder if Grandmother would tell me, Mollie thought, as she lay in bed.

"Mollie, are you dressed yet? We have to leave in ten minutes." Mother's voice sliced through her thoughts. Mollie kicked back her covers, jumped out of bed, and opened her closet door in one motion. Wear something proper—the blue linen. Reed likes it and the weight I've gained won't show. Holly will check out my stomach the minute I walk in. She sucked in her breath. Someday I'll be much thinner than Holly is and she'll fall apart like a house of cards.

"Do I have time for coffee before we go?" Mollie called over the banister to her mother.

"Certainly, dear. Don't gulp it. You don't want to be sick in the car."

"I haven't been sick in the car since I was eight." But I guess it's part of my permanent record, Mollie thought.

"Dear, you must be extra cooperative today."

"Is Grandmother very sick?"

"Of course not." Mother's voice was positive. Mollie stared at her closely.

"What's wrong with her?" Mollie knew she wouldn't get an answer, but she might learn something from Mother's expression.

"Nothing serious."

"Then why all the fuss? You and Dad buzzing in every day, and now me going in."

"You can stay home," Mother said casually.

"Holly going to be there?"

"Yes, Aunt Pat said Holly would be coming down later in the day."

19

"Nate and Robert?"

"I suppose so, Mollie. What does that have to do with it?"

"Nothing, Mother dear. I'm definitely coming." No one was going to keep her from being there if all the other cousins were.

Curled up in the back seat, watching the huge arching trees as Dad drove the car through the winding roads, Mollie strained to hear her parents' conversation. As though she could detect Mollie's intention, Mother turned on the radio, raised the volume, and all Mollie heard was the sugar-laden strings of Mantovani.

Maybe she is Sick, not bad cold or flu, but Sick. Why else all the silence? Mollie uneasily reviewed the possibilities. It hadn't been a heart attack because she had listened carefully every time her father talked to Reed or her uncles on the phone. She had heard no mention of Grandmother's heart. As a matter of fact, she had heard no mention of Grandmother. Most of the conversations had led up to the decision to hire a nurse. Father and Reed assured her it was a measure "to make things easier, make sure the house continues to run smoothly."

But Reed had stopped going downtown. Except for February in Palm Beach and the summer when Grandmother refused to stay in the city, Reed worked every day. Even during Christmas vacation when all the children visited Grandmother, he went to the office for part of the day. He had not been towntown once during the past week.

Mollie glanced out the window. They were flying along the Expressway. No more trees, no more curvy roads. Just no-nonsense cement straightaway. Soon they would be at the apartment, and she could talk with Nate. He might have information about Grandmother. She hoped, he would laugh at her, tell her she was being melodramatic.

As Mollie walked beside her mother into Reed's apartment building, Edward, the doorman, stood up. Mother continued to talk, inclining her head slightly toward Edward. She could say hello to him, instead of acting like he's part of the door, Mollie thought.

She followed Mother into the wood-paneled elevator.

"Don't get in anyone's way, and be as helpful as you can."

"I'll try, Mom."

"Good morning, Reed." Mother was blocking Mollie's view of Reed. "John is parking the car. He'll be right up."

"Reed." Mollie pushed past her mother and hugged her grandfather. He hugged her back. She followed him into the apartment, relieved because he didn't look upset.

"How is Grandmother?"

"Better, I think. The doctor was here earlier. He seems satisfied." Satisfied with what? She hoped Nate was here.

The door to Grandmother's room at the end of the long hall was half closed. Mollie stood quietly, hoping to catch some sound. But all was still.

"Good morning, Country Cousin." Nate looked cheerful. His brother Robert was sitting off by himself, an open book on his lap. Holly was ensconced on the couch, her feet tucked under her, her shoes and some magazines thrown sloppily on the floor beside her.

"Hi, everybody. You look great, Holly."

"Thanks. What have you been up to?" Holly threw another magazine on the pile and smiled at Mollie.

21

"Nothing much." Mollie gathered up the magazines and put them on the coffee table.

"Still seeing David?" Holly asked, flipping through a new magazine so fast the pages blurred in front of Mollie's eyes.

"Slow down, Holl. You'll run out of magazines before the morning's over." Nate was grand. He could say anything to anyone and get away with it. Mollie looked around the room.

"Why is it so dark in here?"

"Because the shades are drawn. And don't try to raise them because Reed will fall apart. He likes it this way. The sunlight seems to disturb him." Holly bit her lip.

"Well, it is his house." Mollie idly traced the brocade fleurs-de-lis on the couch. It did seem strange. All of them dressed up in the middle of the day, in the dim half-light of the formal living room. Each table held a bowl of fresh flowers; there were silver shell-shaped candy dishes set out, as though a party were about to begin. Maybe if they all started talking, it would seem more normal. "Where are your mother and Aunt Cathy?"

"Probably in the kitchen. That iron-willed nurse won't wash a dish or fix so much as a pitcher of lemonade," Holly said.

Mollie walked toward the kitchen, motioning Nate to follow her. She walked slowly, barely moving down the hall, but he didn't appear. She stood in the kitchen doorway, relieved to see Aunt Pat. Mollie had never kept her affection for her aunt a secret. She often told Holly how lucky she was to have Aunt Pat for a mother. She was washing dishes, handing each one to Mother, who waited next to her with a

22

towel. Aunt Cathy lifted bottles out of the refrigerator; all soundlessly. Not a plate clattered on the drainboard, no bottle was allowed to hit the refrigerator shelf. Mollie felt as though she were watching television with the sound turned down. She couldn't hear her cousins talking in the living room, and there was still no sound from Grandmother's room. Maybe I'm losing my hearing, she mused. All these people in the apartment—and no sound.

"Good morning, Aunt Pat," Mollie whispered. "Can I help?" Mollie was delighted to see her aunt. Mother always spoke differently when children were in the room. Aunt Pat talked in the same voice to children, friends, and doormen. Mollie felt freer around this sunny woman, who never got rattled if milk glasses overturned or Holly and Mollie giggled way past bedtime.

"There's nothing to do, dear. Why don't you and Holly go for a walk?"

"It would be better if they stayed here, Pat," Mother said quietly. "After all, they're here to see Grandmother."

Mollie ground her teeth and stalked back to the living room. Where was Reed? Why hadn't Nate come out to the kitchen? She went back to the couch and sat down next to Holly, as Reed entered the living room.

"The nurse thinks it will be all right for each of you children to visit with Grandmother for five minutes. Be very quiet, and don't tire her," he said. "Mollie, why don't you go in first?"

She hoped her nervousness didn't show. Should she act as though Grandmother were just resting? Should she ask how she was feeling, or not mention her illness at all?

Grandmother's peach and silver bedroom. Mollie had

23

never considered this room ordinary. It had a bed, but that was where similarity to other bedrooms ended. The chaise longue, shiny with metallic threads. Grandmother rested there in the afternoons with a peach-colored silk throw over her legs. When they were little, Holly and Mollie were allowed one bounce each on the deliciously soft puff cushion. She wished she were still small, coming into Grandmother's room to bounce on the chaise or to see the rainbows cast on the ceiling by Grandmother's chandelier. It looked like a giant ice cream cone made of icicles. The same crystal icicles hung from the small lamps on Grandmother's bureau. The icicles made a delicate *ping* when Grandmother clicked them together. She used to tell the girls that fairies lived inside the lamps and made the beautiful sound.

As she went into the room, Mollie looked up at the chandelier, expecting the rainbow patterns on the ceiling. But the light was off and the crystal mass hung in the center of the room, as silent as the rest of the apartment. Mollie shivered.

"Good morning, Grandmother." She smiled and stood still, uncertain. Should she sit in a chair or stand at the foot of the bed? Grandmother was wearing a peach-colored long-sleeved nightgown with lace at the wrists and neck. Her hair was braided and wrapped around her head as usual. She didn't look sick except that her freckles seemed like dark pebbles against her pale skin.

"You look fine to me." She has no lips. What happened to her lips? She has no lipstick on. I've never seen Grandmother without lipstick. Mollie chewed her thumbnail.

"Stop chewing your thumb, Mollie. You'll never have pretty hands if you do that."

"Yes, Grandmother." Her voice sounds the same, maybe a little quieter. "Are you tired, Grandmother?"

24

"No, I'm not tired. This jabot is scratching my throat."
She turned to the nurse. "Can't you cut it off?"

The nurse was sitting in a chair to the left of the bed.
There was not supposed to be a chair there. She reached for
a pair of scissors in her white uniform pocket, snipped off
the lace, and returned to her chair. Without a sound. Mollie
smiled at her, but the woman didn't even look at her.

"Will you be able to get up later, Grandmother?"

"As soon as the doctor thinks Mrs. Fields should get up,
she will." The nurse glanced at her watch and motioned to
Mollie. Five minutes were up. Should she kiss Grandmother?

"Come give me a kiss, Mollie." She leaned over her grandmother, taking care not to press too hard on the mattress. As
she kissed the dry cheek, she felt something was wrong,
slightly different, but she couldn't decide what it was. She
smiled. "See you in a little while. Have a nice nap."

Her grandmother turned away from her, sighed, and closed
her eyes.

Mollie walked down the quiet hall to the living room.
Reed was pacing from the library to the kitchen to the living
room. When he saw Mollie, he put his finger to his lips and
motioned her into the room.

"You can go in now, Robert. Don't stay too long and
don't tire Grandmother." Mollie watched Robert lope out
of the room, his shoulders drawn up, his head bent down.
Even when he was walking he looked as though he were
reading. He was so tall and he had a grown man's face now.
He must resent being grouped with us. He should be with
Father and the rest of the men.

Robert was studying molecular biology at MIT and had a
fierceness of purpose that Mollie envied. Robert was going
into research. In his taciturn voice, speaking words Mollie

25

only heard in books, he'd explained to Grandmother that he might find the cure for some killer disease. She had answered that he also might develop this bizarre disease and end up no better than the people he was anxious to cure.

Nate was saying something to Reed, who nodded his head but put his finger to his lips when Nate laughed. Mollie smiled. There was something about Nate that made her feel happy.

He could talk on any subject, easily, whether he knew a lot about it or not. He would make an impressive figure in the courtroom with his tea-colored hair, long stride, and quick smile. They had known for years that Nate would be a lawyer, would join Uncle Rob and Uncle Mike in the office. He was one of the most dashing young men in his class at Harvard.

Walking toward him, she whispered, "Grandmother isn't wearing any lipstick."

"In case nobody mentioned it to you, she's sick," he whispered back, as Reed paced toward the library.

"I've never seen her without lipstick."

"Did she say anything? About how she's feeling?"

"No. She looks OK, except that she's so pale. And that nurse is a zombie. What is she doing there?"

"Making Grandmother's illness official." He grinned.

"Is she that sick, Nate?"

"Well, this isn't a dinner party," he whispered into her ear. Mollie smiled and swallowed her uneasiness.

"Where are Mark and Michael?" They were Holly's younger brothers.

"Home getting ready for camp. Arguing over how many batteries they'll need for their radios or something equally thrilling," Holly said.

"Are they mad they couldn't come?"

"I don't think they know what's happening."

What *is* happening? Mollie wondered, knowing Holly would mangle her if she asked it out loud.

"I said, 'What about Mayhew?' " Holly raised her voice.

"Mom and Dad said he's too young, there would be too many people here, and it wouldn't be appropriate."

"Sounds like Aunt Cyn. Your mother has a deep sense of the appropriate. What did old Mayhew say?"

"He was angry this morning. He wanted to come. It does seem stupid that he can't. As he said to Mother, how can he be too young to see his own grandmother?"

"He can have my place," Holly murmured. When Holly wanted to look bored or disinterested she raised her eyebrows and sucked in her lips the way her father did. But she didn't have the blank expression that Uncle Mike carried off so well. He could freeze any conversation with that look.

Robert came into the room, looking unruffled. The nurse appeared at the door and announced that Grandmother was napping. Mollie felt tears starting. She took a deep breath and clamped her mouth shut. She would not make a spectacle of herself; a Fields did not cry in public. But her cheeks were wet with tears. She hurried from the room, hoping nobody would notice. She ran into the library and collapsed against Reed's desk. As she let her breath out, sobs burst from the back of her throat.

"Mollie, what is this?" Reed was walking toward her and talking softly.

"I'm sorry, Reed," she said, as soon as her breathing was even again. "I didn't mean to cry."

"Of course you didn't. We are all under a great strain." Reed smiled. Mollie wished he would sit down and talk to

27

her alone in the library, but he seemed anxious to leave. If only he would tell her about Grandmother's illness. As he walked toward the door, Mollie searched for a way to ask.

"Reed?"

He turned. "Sit there, dear, until you get control of yourself." He shut the door behind him.

She stroked the arm of the maroon leather chair. There was a picture of her and Nate and Holly as little children sitting in that chair, mostly legs dangling in the air, and huge smiles as they looked directly into the camera. The picture was so familiar to Mollie that she looked down at the chair surprised. There were only a couple of inches on each side of her. Had the three of them really fit so snugly into the chair? She could remember everything they had done as children, but she couldn't remember being so small.

If only the three of them had sat in the chair every few months—used it as a kind of yardstick—then she could have caught the moment when they had grown too big for the chair, had started to become different people.

Mollie stood up and smoothed her dress, and raked at her hair with Reed's antique letter opener. Would she ever be able to please them, to reach the point where she automatically did the right thing?

Chapter Three

"Hang your dress in the closet so it doesn't get wrinkled," Mollie said. Hilary was spending the night because Mollie's parents were staying at Aunt Pat's. Mollie stretched out across her bed and watched Hilary pull clothes from her suitcase. Hilary chattered away as she hung up her daisy-printed dress, one sleeve dangling from the hanger. She tossed her shoes behind her onto the closet floor, knocking apart Mollie's neatly paired shoes, and impatiently pawed through the mixture in her suitcase. She soon covered half the bed and Mollie's legs with a chain necklace, earrings, underwear, a pair of calico-patched jeans, a nightgown, a heap of blouses, sticks of makeup, two handfuls of bobby pins, and a plastic bag bulging with rollers.

"Hilary, did you leave anything at home?" Mollie shrugged the clothes off her legs and began arranging the items in piles on her bed.

"I wasn't sure what I'd feel like wearing tonight." Mollie marveled at her friend's inability to worry. Several months before Senior Prom, Mollie asked Hilary what she would do if no one asked her to the dance. Mollie was already anticipating that crisis for herself. How embarrassed she would be. But Hilary laughed.

"I'll take my brother. Or maybe Hew. He's been to dancing school, hasn't he?"

"What a terrific day," Mollie now said suddenly. She felt so relaxed, so free. For the first time since Reed's call two weeks ago, she would have a two-day vacation from the recurring picture of Grandmother lying so still in that room. Hew was staying with Porky for the weekend. Her parents had allowed her to stay home as long as Hilary came and she wouldn't be in the house alone. She and Hilary had the house to themselves! No one to check what time she and David got home; no fear of waking her parents in the middle of the night with laughter, the slamming of the front door.

"Isn't this a neat belt?" Hilary held up a wide silver belt, pieces of decorated metal tied together with strips of rough leather. Mollie didn't care for its homemade look, but she nodded her approval. After the tension at Reed's apartment, she didn't want a shadow of discord during the weekend.

"Eddie has a friend who makes them. We went to visit him the other day and he gave it to me. He said he can always add another link if I get fat."

"That was a safe offer."

"He lives way out in the country past Pleasantville. He got together with these other guys, and they're farming, on a small piece of land, and they make jewelry. . . ."

"Are there half-naked little kids playing in the mud?"

"It's near Pleasantville, not Appalachia or Bangladesh."

"Scratch the muddy kids then." Mollie paused for a minute. "But they are doing the dropout scene, right?"

"Cut it out, Mollie. You sound like Holly and her crowd. The swollen-tongue sophisticates."

"How does Eddie know them?" Mollie slid right over Hilary's remark. She didn't want any hassles. She didn't know much about Hilary's latest boy. Eddie always greeted her with a slow lazy smile and a slithery "How you gettin' on, baby?" that made her cheeks burn.

The way he slouched down in her parents' living room with an army fatigue cap tilted over his eyes, he could have been sitting on the beach or under a tree. He was oblivious to the pale upholstery and had no idea of the ultimata Mollie had received about keeping that filthy boy out of the living room.

"They were in the same class. We were driving around near where they live and Eddie wanted to see how they were getting along, so we went over." Hilary looked at her suitcase and dropped it on the floor. "Might as well leave the rest in there."

"Want to hit the club this aft?" Mollie asked. Hilary had her own tan Vega, just a shade darker than her hair. She managed, even in her slapdash way, to end up color-coordinated. Sometimes Mollie suspected that her super-casual friend was stronger and tougher than Holly, who gave the impression of a metal structure, immune to weather or other outside influences.

"I'd better wash my hair. I'm walking grease." She touched a strand of hair and wiped her hand on her shirt with a look of disgust. "Where are you and David going?"

31

"Probably the band concert in the park. All the movies stink. I think they're having a Disney retrospective at the Playhouse." Mollie giggled. "What about you and Edwardo?"

"Who knows?"

"Why not come with us?" Mollie asked. It had been a long time since they had double-dated.

"I don't think so."

"Why not?"

"No reason." Hilary's voice trailed off. Her face got tight. Mollie said in an offhand tone, "Anything wrong? Don't you and Eddie like David?" They probably didn't.

Mollie wasn't wild about him herself. He was pleasant though, and her parents liked him. He looked like the boys in *Glamour* and *Mademoiselle*. Every time she went out with him, she felt as though she had done something good —like calling her great-aunt or finishing every bit of homework in every single subject.

"It has nothing to do with David." Mollie didn't push it. Hilary frowned. She seemed to be struggling with something; Mollie and she had been friends since first grade, and Hilary's face and reactions were so predictable to Mollie that any alteration in Hilary's carefree manner jarred. Hilary had been concerned about something for the past few weeks. Mollie guessed it had something to do with Eddie. She was hurt that Hilary didn't tell her. Mollie was afraid that Eddie might separate them. Hilary was the only person Mollie could tell everything to. She was the only one Mollie discussed her family with. When Mollie felt isolated from the family, Hilary made her feel good again.

"How's your grandmother?" Hilary asked.

"She's still sick, but they say she's getting stronger. Dad thought she looked better yesterday. She still looks pale to me. We've all been there every day this week, even Dad, Reed, and my uncles. But she seemed better yesterday. So Aunt Pat suggested we take the weekend off, so to speak. Aunt Pat's great!"

"What's wrong with your grandmother?"

"I don't know."

"You don't know!" Hilary shouted. "What do your parents say?"

"Nothing. Just that we have to do our best and cooperate."

"What does that mean?"

"How the hell should I know? I've begun to think that maybe she's . . . she's . . ." Mollie couldn't say the word.

"What about Reed?"

"He looks lousy. Exceedingly grim. But he looks that way whenever anything's wrong with Grandmother. Remember two years ago when she broke her ankle in the Tuscan hills?"

"When Reed chartered the plane to bring her back?"

"Yes. He insisted on bringing her every meal tray himself, and when we went to visit, he kept shushing us. That's how it is now."

"Like talking would shatter a broken ankle." Hilary shook her head and snorted. "Your family's love of secrecy . . ."

Hilary was the only outsider who half understood her family. But Mollie couldn't explain how much these remarks hurt her, since she had realized a long time ago she couldn't change the family and their rules!

"Sorry, Moll. I didn't mean to put down his being upset. It's just frustrating that you can't glean any details about what's wrong.

"Hil, let's just drop it. I want to forget the whole mess

33

this weekend." Hilary had said out loud what had been whispering through Mollie's mind since she had first seen Grandmother lying in bed, surrounded by a soundless family.

"What about Nate? Holly? What do they think?"

"Holly has a sore throat. She's been in bed the past few days."

"I'll just bet." Hilary raised her eyebrows.

"Cool it; she's really sick."

"Holly has a terrible sore throat, Moll. Probably diphtheria. Why don't you admit it? She avoids anything unpleasant. When those guys were killed last summer on Stony Brook Bridge, and your cousin had been dating one of them for a year, who was the only no-show at the memorial service?"

"She was too upset to go," Mollie said.

"She probably had nothing to wear," Hilary said. "It was awfully short notice."

"Why are you so cruddy about Holly? She's always been nice to you."

"Because you don't see her in any light except a holy one. What's so great about her? Except that she's part of your sacred family."

"What's so *un*great about her?"

"Nothing. I don't care one way or the other about Holly. I just get steamy when you quote her like some unerring oracle."

"Let's forget it. You don't know her except what you hear from me."

"And it ain't good," Hilary muttered.

Mollie got off the bed and looked through the closet for something to wear that night. She was tired of trying to make

34

explanations to Hilary. It was impossible because Hilary's family was so different. Her parents never made a commotion if she came home late or left the kitchen a mess after midnight snacks. Mollie had to watch out for these things—but she had to make sure her friends didn't notice her concern about it.

Mollie zipped up her dress and reached for a comb. Hilary continued alternately chewing on an apple and filing her fingernails. She was sitting in her underwear in no hurry to get dressed.

"Eddie'll be here soon, Hil, and you won't be dressed."

"Horrors. Your hair looks fine; stop fiddling with it."

"Are you going to get dressed, or do you plan to go out in your underwear?"

"I'll see when I finish my apple."

The doorbell rang, and Mollie said, "It must be Eddie because David said eight."

"Maybe he's early."

Mollie shook her head. "When David says *eight*, he means eight. He's never early, never late."

"How dull." Hilary took a final bite of apple.

"At least I know when to be dressed." The bell rang again.

"Well, whoever it is, I'm not dressed as you can see. So you'd better let the mystery caller in." Hilary's face had flushed and she was moving rapidly toward the closet.

"What should I say?"

"Offer him an apple." Hilary laughed. "C'mon, Mollie; talk to him like he was plain old Eddie Schumacher."

Mollie opened the door, hoping that it was, by some fluke, David, early.

35

"How you gettin' on, baby?"

"Hello, Eddie; how great to see you." He smelled sweaty; Mollie was glad her parents weren't home.

"Where's Petunia?"

"Petunia?"

"Sure. Hilary looks less like a petunia than any girl I know." He sat on the couch with his feet on the coffee table, his shoe resting against a porcelain robin. "I dated a girl once who used to get snowed when I called her flower names. I told Hilary about it one night and well . . . Petunia."

"How cute." What was taking Hilary so long? "Hilary told me you visited this guy who dr—who lives near Pleasantville. The guy who gave her the belt," Mollie added when Eddie's face remained blank. Maybe he wasn't listening.

"Old Mike? Yeah, he left school last year. Seems to dig what he's doing. Anything beats school. Right, baby?" He smiled slowly and Mollie crossed her legs.

"How'll he ever get a job?"

Eddie shrugged and the bird tottered. Mollie got up and casually moved it to the corner of the table. "He's a brilliant guy. He'll get a job later if he wants one."

"Would you like some beer?"

"Well, that depends." He leaned forward and bellowed, "Petunia? You have a date with some other guy tonight?" He probably wore ripped undershirts.

"I'll be down in a sec. Have a beer?"

"You heard the lady." He smiled at Mollie through slitty eyes and she left the room quickly.

As she was bringing Eddie his beer, the doorbell rang. It was exactly eight o'clock. Mollie shouted, "Hilary!"

"In a minute."

36

Mollie set the beer can on a magazine on the table. David. Clean David. It was reassuring to look at him.

"Hi. How come all the upstairs lights are on? Thought your parents were in town."

"Hilary's staying, and she's still up there. You want a beer? Eddie's having one."

David looked at his watch. "A quick one. I told Meg and Tom we'd meet them at the park at eight forty-five."

Should she get David's beer, or give Eddie his now? What was Hilary doing up there? Eddie reached for the beer can and then shook hands with David. I bet he wouldn't have done that if David hadn't held out his hand first, Mollie thought on her way back to the kitchen.

"Hilary, do you want a beer?"

"Why are you screaming? I'm right behind you." Mollie jerked around and saw Hilary, her hair piled high on her head, some hanging to her shoulders, looking like a Victorian maiden in her long ruffled dress.

"How can you get so dressed up that fast?" Mollie said, exasperated. No matter how long she worked at it, she always looked the same.

"This is the easiest dress in the world. Hides a multitude of sins," she said. "Can't even tell where I scraped off half my leg shaving."

"You girls going to huddle in there all night?" Eddie called.

"Not hardly," Hilary sang as they walked through the door.

Mollie stared at Eddie as he set his beer can on the table. What a slob. An eighteenth-century table. Her mother would explode.

They'd think she was a jerk if she started slipping coasters under beer cans. I hope it doesn't leave a ring, she thought morosely.

"We'd better hit the road, Mollie." David stood in front of the fireplace, one hand in his pants pocket, and the other resting lightly on the mantel. "Good to see you, Schumacher. Good night, Hilary." He flicked a speck of lint off his jacket and smiled broadly at Mollie. She had asked him once why he always wore a jacket when they went out at night. He answered that he did it out of respect for her. David said things that were utterly quotable to Grandmother. With some boys Mollie had to alter conversations to make the boy seem acceptable, but David was verbatim acceptable.

Chapter Four

At twelve o'clock David brought her home.

"Good night, Mollie. See you at the club tomorrow?" David opened the front door and Mollie stepped inside.

"Probably Hil and I will come over around noon. Since Dad is away, we can sleep late." She smiled happily. She watched David walk straight down the driveway. He never walked across the grass. Would he ever hurl a rock at the maple tree on the way back to his car or bay at the moon or run back to tell her a funny thought? No, straight down the driveway, as he had done a hundred times before.

Well, I can't crunch him for that, Mollie reminded herself. That's his biggest asset. Dependable, steady, no surprises. David had dispelled many of her uncertainties about boys, her fears about having dates for key occasions and finding a boy who would please the family. David was always around, always made arrangements for dances and parties weeks in advance, and was "the answer to a mother's prayers," as Mother had proudly described him to Aunt Pat. He wasn't daring or exotic, like Holly's young men, but he was eminently presentable and didn't take up too much of Mollie's time. She didn't have strong feelings about him, didn't think about him at all when he wasn't around. She was relieved that they never had dramatic arguments or hysterical fights. David was not a world-beater, not a headliner, but Mollie was grateful that he was so predictable. He would never desert her.

Mollie looked toward the stairs. Hilary didn't seem to be back yet. Or else she had gone to sleep, highly unlikely since she was a *Late Late Show* addict and sat up most nights watching fading westerns. Mollie went upstairs, hoping Hilary would come home soon. Half the fun of a date was to be able to talk about it later. Hilary knew everything that had ever happened between Mollie and David, knew practically every word they had ever spoken to each other. Hilary would collapse when Mollie described David at the concert, leaning back with his eyes closed, pretending to lead the band, his left hand swooping and skipping along, making small birdlike motions in the air. And how he tasted so strongly of peppermint Lifesavers when they kissed. Hilary and Mollie always laughed about that.

Mollie wandered from room to room, wishing Hilary would hurry and come home. It was so quiet; maybe she should have asked David to stay and watch television. But she had been counting on Hilary to be waiting. There had been people around since Grandmother had become ill, and Mollie didn't like roaming the house, alone with her uncertain thoughts. She got undressed slowly, picked up a book, and got into bed to kill time until Hilary returned. She

40

flipped pages, peeked at the end, read a few pages in the middle, decided she had gleaned enough of the story, threw it down, and looked around for something else to do. But she could think of only one logical activity at two o'clock in the morning—sleep. So she left a note for Hilary, "Wake me if you want to talk," and resolutely went to sleep.

Mollie woke up, but saw no light in the hall. Four o'clock. Hilary must have gone directly to bed. Mollie, scarcely awake, burrowed deeper into her pillow and slid back into sleep.

A slight noise, a whispering, a creaking. Mollie dragged herself awake and saw from the dim half-light that it was barely morning. A rustling, a whisper. She heard it again. Mollie couldn't identify the sound but it was seeping into her consciousness. Could it have been part of a dream? She sat up in bed, listening. Someone or something was moving; Mollie knew that was ridiculous. She and Hilary were the only people in the house and Hilary was asleep in Hew's room. Father was right; she had an overactive imagination. As she heard the noise again, she decided it must be the bamboo shade knocking against the kitchen window. I'd better get up and fix it, or I'll never get back to sleep. Why this morning of all mornings? Any other day Dad would be home, would go down and fix the loose shade, and Mollie could fall back asleep. She sighed and went into the hall.

Halfway down the stairs she stopped short. She must be dreaming. Hilary was closing the front door. What was she doing down there, sliding the lock closed ever so slowly? Maybe the flapping window shade had awakened her too and she was looking for the cause of the noise? The morning newspaper? Before dawn?

Mollie struggled against considering any other possibilities.

She needed time. She tiptoed back to bed, not ready to confront Hilary. She pulled her quilt tight around her, wishing she could erase the picture of Hilary standing at the door in her short fluffy nightgown.

She trusted Hilary, but . . . She tossed off the covers, forced into action because her thoughts had reached a dead end and could only repeat themselves over and over, like a car spinning its wheels in a snowdrift.

She went into the bathroom, left the door open, and turned the taps on full force in the tub. Then she dropped a plastic glass on the floor and waited. Hilary appeared at the door.

"God, you're up early." She's acting as if nothing happened. She probably didn't see me standing there. I can't trust her. She must have . . . Mollie said nothing.

"I'm going back to sleep for a while. I'm still tired."

Mollie waited a minute, as if she hadn't heard Hilary, then said, "I guess you would be."

Hilary bit her lip and said softly, "Let's talk later. I'm really tired."

That did it. "Isn't that too goddamn bad! I'm wide awake. I *slept* all night."

"OK, I get the point." Hilary looked miserable.

"How could you do this to me?" Mollie was surprised that her voice came out in a scream. She hadn't planned to scream. Her hands were shaking.

"To you?"

"Yes. If my parents had come home unexpectedly . . . they trusted you . . . I trusted you . . . you were my best friend . . ." Mollie couldn't go on. She gripped the sink tightly, afraid that she might hit Hilary in her rage.

42

"Cool down, Mollie. You sound like somebody's mother."

"I thought you were my friend," Mollie repeated.

"We are friends. This has nothing to do with you." Mollie sucked in her breath. She had been right about Eddie. She had been cut out; he had driven a wedge between her and Hilary. They had always shared everything. Their friendship had reached its end. Mollie narrowed her eyes, compressed her lips, and bent over the tub. Hilary would not be able to see how completely sliced apart she felt.

"Let's talk about it later, Moll." Hilary attempted to hug her as she left the bathroom, but Mollie pulled away and turned her head. "I can't explain . . . it's just . . . I thought you might . . ." Hilary sighed, slumped forward, and wearily shook her head. Mollie was glad she seemed so confused. And Mollie was not about to make it easier for her.

Mollie hadn't even suspected. She reviewed the last few weeks: Hilary's actions, their conversations. Had there been hints Mollie had been too dumb to catch? And why hadn't Hilary told her? That was the killing part. Why hadn't she trusted her? Mollie knew she was a loyal friend; knew she had never let Hilary down. So why had Hilary become secretive?

Petunia. Eddie had said he had been calling Hilary that for a while. Maybe that was part of it, a code word. Hilary had never mentioned it to her. They had never kept secrets from one another. Hilary even knew about Mollie's family.

Hilary had used her. She had pretended she wanted to spend the weekend with Mollie but what she really wanted was a place to meet Eddie, to stay with him. Mollie felt sick, limp, and helpless. The bath water was turning cold, but she didn't have the energy to get out of the tub.

43

Grandmother lying in bed, Reed pacing from room to room and only half-noticing the people around him, unavailable to Mollie. And Hilary. Leading a secret life that excluded Mollie. Even as she felt herself hating Hilary, she struggled against it. She couldn't face being alone.

Why did things have to change? Just when she understood, felt in control of situations, they changed, and she had to start over again. New rules, new patterns. She thought of Holly's backyard, and the marvelous wooden playhouse, set back from the house, half hidden by two arching copper beech trees. From those Mollie Make-Believe days when she fit each cousin into a role, even the playhouse had been given a part. One Sunday Robert was running through the door to tell Holly, the Indian princess, that they had captured Caddie Woodlawn, when *smack*—his forehead slammed against the doorframe. He had grown too tall! After that day he paused every time he entered the playhouse. Soon the games changed; no role for Robert and the playhouse seemed smaller. It was abandoned to the younger cousins. Occasionally Mollie and Holly would sneak in and crouch on the floor to tell secrets; just the two of them filling up the playhouse. It was hard to imagine they had believed in the tiny house as a huge pioneer cabin, a real house with a sign on the door: NO GROWN-UPS ALLOWED.

Mollie wished her parents would come home. She longed to hear her father complaining that Mollie slept half the day away. She wanted her mother to tell her to put her shoes on. She wanted to yell at Hew for not cleaning the sink after he brushed his teeth. Maybe she could pretend to be asleep all day, and Hilary would go home. Then Mollie could get up, her parents would come home, and everything would be normal again. After all she wasn't sure. She had drawn her conclusion about Hilary just from seeing her at the door in her nightgown.

No wonder Hilary hadn't wanted to discuss it. Mollie had been horrid. I'll apologize right now. Then we can have a big breakfast, maybe go to the movies, and everything will be OK. Mollie went toward Hew's room. The sooner this whole thing could be forgotten, the better.

Hilary sat up in bed. "I'm sorry, Moll. We shouldn't have . . ."

"Hilary, it's my fault. I should have given you a chance to explain. Let's forget it and have breakfast."

"What I'm sorry about is that we used your house without telling you. But, well, we didn't plan . . ."

Mollie cut her off. "What do you mean? You mean what I saw was *right*?" The hollow feeling was back.

"All you saw was me in a nightgown."

"Don't play games. Admit it straight out."

"I slept with Eddie," Hilary said.

"You're gross!" Mollie said, and ran out of the room.

Mollie lay shivering on her back, trying to draw warmth from her quilt. Her anger toward Hilary had given way to terror. Finally it had come, that time that had seemed so distant. Hilary had deserted their magazine-slick dating life. She had ended those nights of mutual laughter, when they had described their dates to each other, those later-night discussions that were so often more fun than the dates themselves. Hilary had silenced the words they had said to each other for so long, "I know what you mean." Hilary had slipped into this world they considered a shadowy specter far ahead of them, a world of mystery they dismissed with minimal curiosity for "later."

Tears fell down Mollie's cheeks as she rolled over and hugged her pillow. Hilary had all that knowledge now, she had become a shadow herself, and suddenly Mollie was desperate to catch up, to rejoin her friend. But the dim shadows grew even darker and more menacing as Mollie tried to reach toward them.

David! Her stomach knotted. She didn't want to touch his body. She didn't want to be undressed in front of him. She gasped. The chasm between her and Hilary was wider than she had realized. It was back to choosing teams again, and Hilary had gone over to the other side. Leaving Mollie alone.

Chapter Five

M ollie approached the ivory-and-gold painted door of her grandparents' apartment with dread. The routine was becoming automatic. Everyone so still, so unnaturally quiet. The low hum of the air conditioners making it easy to forget the hot stickiness outside.

It always seemed to be the same day, the same time inside.

The shades were drawn halfway, holding back the sun; the small table lamps were lit, casting a quieter light. The family took up their same places each morning. Mollie sat on the floor, leaning against Nate's chair; the couch had been relinquished to Aunt Cathy and Mollie's mother. They sat silently, each working on a needlepoint canvas, their hands creating a constant rhythm as more of the intricate pattern was revealed each day. A pile of brightly colored yarn was heaped between them. Only Reed, pacing from Grandmother's room into the living room or into the library where his sons were stationed, broke the tableau.

Mollie tried to take comfort from the presence of her father and uncles as they gathered around Reed, planning in muted voices. She whispered to Nate; she emptied her mother's ashtray every couple of hours. She waited for Aunt Pat to send her on an errand, give her a task from the list she carried around as she poked into closets and cupboards and moved among the other adults, adding to her list of details hastily printed on a yellow legal pad. Aunt Pat was the only one who smiled at Mollie when she passed.

But nothing dissolved the panic lodged in Mollie's throat, lumped in her stomach. She knew now that Grandmother was very ill. She might die. None of them discussed it; her parents, her cousins, Reed, all kept the secret. An occasional cough from Grandmother's room and the loud silence of the whole family, usually so talkative, were the only reminders of why they were here.

When Mother's parents had died, Mollie had been ten. She had heard Mother crying late one night. She had gotten out of bed and wandered down the long hall to her parents' room. Her father had told her to go back to bed.

"Why is Mommy crying?" Mollie had stood in the doorway, whispering to him as though her mother were not in the room.

"Gram and Grampa have been in an accident. Mother and I will be leaving for Boston early in the morning."

"OK. Will you kiss me good night, Daddy?"

"C'mon back to bed. I hope you will be a good girl and not give Edna any trouble while we're gone."

"I'll be good and I promise not to fight with Hew even if he kicks me first." She had kissed her father's nose, her special place.

"That's my girl."

A couple of days later Edna had told her and Hew that their grandparents had died in the hospital. Mollie had called Reed to get some more information.

"Reed, will Mother and Daddy be home soon?"

"Yes, dear, as soon as the funeral is over."

"Can we go to the funeral?"

"Of course not, Mollie. A funeral is no place for a child."

"When can I go to one?"

"Let's hope not for a very long time." Reed had laughed, so Mollie had laughed too.

When her parents got home, they didn't mention the funeral. They brought Mollie a charm bracelet of Gram's, but Mother said she couldn't wear it until she was older. Mollie had followed Daddy upstairs.

"What did you do there?" she asked as he snapped open his suitcase.

"Mollie, it's not the sort of thing you discuss. It is very sad, and we shall all miss Gram and Grampa very much. But life goes on," he added as he hung up his navy blazer.

She decided to give it one last try before the subject was sealed away forever. "Did you see them dead?"

"What did I just say?" He walked over to the chair in which Mollie was sitting and looked down at her sternly. Her father had definitely closed the discussion.

"I'm sorry," she had said. But now she'd never find out. It didn't seem right to ask Mother since it had been *her* parents who died.

Mollie didn't miss those grandparents particularly. She hadn't seen them very often and didn't think about them unless it was her birthday or Christmas. They had always sent her good presents and she had always written them prompt thank-you notes. Since she couldn't picture them dead, it simply seemed as though they had stopped visiting and sending presents.

But Grandmother. Mollie talked to her several times a week and often held conversations with her in her head. She figured in every part of Mollie's life. She knew who Mollie's friends were, what grades she got, what clothes she bought, what teachers she had trouble with, what boys she was seeing. She knew Grandmother's thought about almost every event in Mollie's life. When she got well, Mollie could tell her about Hilary. Grandmother's firmness, her conviction that she was right, always helped Mollie decide what to do. If only she could talk to Grandmother, she'd know how to act with Hilary.

It had always worked. Early last year Mollie had been secretly hoping to go to the Junior Prom with Mickey Stevens. Holly had agreed that Mickey would probably ask her. From then on Mollie began to plan for the dance, as a certainty with Mickey her date. When, three weeks before the dance, Rosemarie Dubrow had told everyone she was going to the prom with Mickey, Mollie had been crushed. She had already bought a new dress, new shoes. She had hinted to her friends. How could she admit that he hadn't asked her?

Mollie avoided the subject with her parents and even with Hilary, but the ache grew inside her, spreading down from her stomach into her legs, making it painful to walk sometimes, especially around school where the only topic discussed was the dance, now a week away.

Finally when she thought she would burst, Mollie told Grandmother.

"And he's—he's going with Rosemarie." Mollie looked down at the floor, as though she could see her humiliation spread out at Grandmother's feet.

"Then you certainly don't want to go with him," Grandmother said decisively, her hands never moving from her lap. "And don't you let anyone know that you are disappointed. Hold your head high." She paused and waited until Mollie raised her head and looked her in the eye. "Act as though you couldn't care less. You must learn to roll with the punches; you mustn't let little things disturb you."

"But he's the boy I wanted to go with," Mollie answered feebly.

Grandmother sat silently for a moment. "You will go to the dance with a friend of Nate's. All the girls will be jealous. They will be with the same ordinary boys they see every day. But you will have a special boy, a new face. A boy none of the girls know." Grandmother had solved it all.

"You can go in and say hello to Grandmother, Mollie." Reed was standing next to her, wearing the jacket he had worn yesterday. He usually changed his clothes twice a day, always wore a fresh shirt for dinner. She looked up at him and smiled. He was so strong! He would be ashamed of her if he knew how she dreaded these five-minute visits with Grandmother. Everyone else was glad to see Grandmother, and their reaction if they found out how much Mollie hated seeing Grandmother in that bed was unthinkable.

Please, God, don't let her die.

"Is Grandmother feeling better this morning?" she asked, as she stood up and smoothed her dress.

"She does seem somewhat stronger today, dear."

Maybe Grandmother wouldn't die after all. Oh God, if only she would get well soon.

She walked quickly into the peach-colored room. The sharp smell of alcohol mixed with the flat impersonal powder the nurse used after bathing Grandmother. So different from the spicy, slightly sweet smell in the room before the illness. Mollie's eyes darted from sign to sign, checking for the now-familiar items: the row of squat, amber-colored medicine bottles on the bureau where the crystal perfume bottles had stood; the nurse to the left of the bed in a stiff chair from the library; Grandmother lying against a mass of pillows—her head small against their fluffy whiteness. Everything was as it had been yesterday. Mollie could detect no ominous signs, and Reed had said that Grandmother seemed stronger.

As she approached the bed, Mollie took a deep breath. "Good morning, Grandmother. It's a lovely day."

Her grandmother didn't answer. Her eyes stayed closed. Had Mollie said the wrong thing? She looked across to the nurse for guidance, but her face was half-hidden by the morning newspaper. Maybe Grandmother hadn't heard her. "Good morning, Grandmother," she said softly. Grandmother didn't move. Her eyes stayed closed, her body perfectly straight under the sheet. She must have drifted off to sleep, Mollie thought.

She turned to leave. Grandmother spoke. "Don't be nervous, Mollie. There's nothing to be frightened of." She hadn't moved and she hadn't opened her eyes.

"I'm not frightened. I'll see you later, Grandmother. The nurse wants me to leave now." As she left the room, Mollie felt the sweat under her armpits. Her hands were shaking.

She collapsed onto the kitchen stool. Even when Grandmother was so terribly ill, even with her eyes closed, she knew what Mollie was thinking.

"Are you all right, dear? I hope you're not catching what Holly has." Aunt Pat's brisk voice was like a rough washcloth bringing feeling back to her face.

"I'm fine."

"Why don't you take a walk, clear your head?" She put her hand on Mollie's shoulder. "Go up and see Holly. She must be bored all alone in the apartment."

"No, really. I'm fine."

Mother came into the kitchen.

"I told her to go visit Holly, get some air." Aunt Pat moved toward the sink, tying an apron around her waist. Mother started piling coffee cups into the sink. Mollie leaned back on her stool and watched the two women. From the back they could have been sisters, both tall, with shoulder-length gray-brown hair combed high away from their foreheads and caught in the back with tortoiseshell barrettes. Both wearing pastel sweaters over their shoulders, the same shade of nail polish, similar gold and diamond pins on their sleeveless knit dresses. Mollie called Mother's pin the instant-replay pin. Uncle Mike had given Aunt Pat her pin about three years ago, and Mother had hinted for one too. She had finally gotten the pin, feigned complete surprise as she opened the package, and even Dad reacted, as Mother kept insisting that she hadn't had the slightest inkling about the pin. Maybe that's why I think of them as being similar, Mollie thought. They dress the same way and Mother certainly tries to do whatever Aunt Pat does. But Aunt Pat knows what she wants to do, has an instinct for making choices. Mother doesn't. No wonder Holly is so different from me.

"Why don't you go, dear?"

"Good idea, Mom. If you're sure it's all right," she added automatically.

"Stay up there for the afternoon and we'll pick you up on the way home."

"Do you think Reed will be hurt?"

"He's got so much on his mind, he probably won't even notice." Aunt Pat winked at her. If she believes that, she doesn't know him at all, Mollie thought as she went into the living room. Nate and Robert were both engrossed in books, looking as calm as though they were in a library. Reed went to the door with her.

She touched his sleeve. "Is it OK, I mean, to leave?" She looked at him intently.

"Of course, dear. You need some air."

"I don't like to leave Grandmother," she said, searching for a reaction.

"Of course you don't. But she will be sleeping most of the day and won't miss you."

"All right, but tomorrow I'll be here all day." She reached up to hug him good-bye. He squeezed her and kissed the top of her head, the way he had for as long as she could remember. And it seemed impossible that Grandmother was ill, that Mollie was old enough to be going away to school, that everything wasn't the way it had always been.

When she walked through the lobby, the doorman jumped up from his bench and saluted her formally. Mollie remembered how she and Holly, when they were little, used to sit on his bench and talk to him while Grandmother took her afternoon nap upstairs. Nothing stayed the same!

54

"Good morning, Miss Mollie. How is Mrs. Fields this morning?"

"She seems a lot stronger, thank you, Edward."

"Shall I get you a taxi, Miss?"

"No thank you, I'll walk."

"We're all so concerned about Mrs. Fields." Edward tipped his hat.

"We appreciate it, Edward," she said as she swept through the door. I sound like Mother, Mollie thought sadly.

She merged into the stream of people walking downtown. It had been such an awful few weeks. Father was more silent than usual—moving like a windup toy, driving the car, talking to his brothers, moving about the living room, straightening magazines, but not speaking to anyone unless necessary.

And the gap, where Hilary's voice should have been comforting her. Each time Mollie felt the urge to call Hilary, she reminded herself that it was Hilary who had broken their mutual trust. Hilary, her best friend. They could never be friends the way they had been before. Even the certainty of David's nightly call was gone. Just the thought of him had begun to make Mollie queasy and seeing him had become unbearably embarrassing. After that night when she had found out about Hilary and Eddie, Mollie had tried to avoid David. But his loyalty and persistence made that impossible. Finally unable to tolerate his presence Mollie told him that she wouldn't be able to see him anymore—hinting that the family thought it better at least until Grandmother was well again. David took the news calmly and had called only twice—to inquire after Grandmother. Mollie was surprised that she felt a tremendous release, as though her slate were now wiped clean, a fresh fall blackboard waiting for her at Springfield.

She was heading toward the park. She crossed the plaza to watch the ice-cream peddlers and vendors. Shaggy men selling tacos, Italian ices, souvlaki—they were all newcomers, cashing in on the traditional Good-Humor stand. As she cut across the scarred, scorched ground, she tripped over a tree root. New York trees were different from country ones. Here the roots grew partially exposed as though there was not enough earth for them to sink into. There was no dense green grass in the city for people or trees. She found a thick, twisted, butterscotch-colored root rising out of the ground, big enough to sit on. Mollie brushed off the root and looked around to make sure that no one was heading toward the same tree. Just a few pigeons searching the ground for old Cracker-Jack kernels. She could watch the scene undisturbed.

A flurry of children ran by, their small arms stretched as high as possible, each one trying to make his Mickey-Mouse balloon float the closest to the sky. She and Holly used to do that, over the same cobblestones. Careful not to run too far from Grandmother's bench. Careful not to let go of the string, wrapped many times around her hand because if this one floated away, she would not get another balloon. Mollie had clutched her string so tightly it seemed to become part of her fist. After hot chocolate and bakery cookies, she had carried her treasure home and wound the string around her lamp.

Mollie grimaced. The balloon, shrinking slightly each day, the color becoming deeper, the black face markings heavier. Until finally the balloon fell limp, dangling from the lamp, all its air gone. Just a shapeless skin to be thrown away. Mollie began to cry. *Let go of the string.* She flopped over, her head in her lap, drew her knees up, and cried harder as the image seeped through her. No one could see her, she could cry as long as she wanted. *Let go.* She looked up into the flat blue sky, imagining Grandmother floating above the park, disappearing into the sky as full-blown and forceful as she had always been.

As the picture lost its power over her, Mollie wiped her face on the backs of her hands, and slipped on her sunglasses. A boy with shoulder-length dark hair wearing tight faded jeans was laughing with the ice-cream man as he tore the paper from his ice cream. Mollie stared at him, her eyes tired from crying. She liked his relaxed manner. Grandmother would shake her head at how unkempt he was. Nate and Robert had never tried anything more unusual than below-the-ears hair, and Uncle Rob used to tease them about not having the money for a haircut. She knew they'd never be allowed to indulge in a look that was a radical departure from what the family expected. She wondered if they wanted to. She was startled to see the boy walking toward her.

"Mind if I sit here? Ice cream melts slower in the shade."

"Sure." Mollie nodded her head. She was too tired to move. And what could happen in the middle of a summer day with hundreds of people crisscrossing the plaza and all the vendors lining the entrance to the park? The boy settled himself on the ground, arranged his muddy-colored canvas pack under his feet, and leaned against the tree. Probably sits that way in living rooms, like Eddie, Mollie thought.

"I'm Jaimie Hart." He looked at Mollie.

"I'm Mollie Fields." She tried to match his inflection.

"You must live close by and are going to a party. Either that or you're a tourist."

"What makes you think that?"

"The way you're dressed. Tourists dress up in the city no matter how much walking they're going to do, no matter how hot it is. It's either respect for tall buildings or fear of the concrete." He paused and took a lick of his ice cream. "Or you live right around here and are stopping at the plaza for a minute. You certainly didn't plan to go walking in the park, not in that linen dress and those cramped shoes."

"You're very observant," she answered weakly.

"Am I right, do you live around here?"

She smiled. "No, I live in the suburbs. And I'm not afraid of concrete and I think tall buildings are just short buildings that have grown."

"Touché." He shook his head. "Clichés get me every time." They both laughed. Mollie noticed the red highlights of the sun in his hair.

He saw her looking at him and asked, "Would you like an ice cream, little girl?"

Mollie hesitated. "Toasted almond, all right?" he asked as he got up, carefully resting his pack under the tree. Mollie reached for her pocketbook but Jaimie was striding toward the ice-cream vendor. Should she let him pay for it? He seemed fine, not stoned or crazy, and the family would never know. Mollie felt her mood changing suddenly; her sadness had turned inside out. She could almost believe the sun was shining deep inside her. This is what Springfield would be like. She would be free to act her own way.

Jaimie was walking toward her. He had a strong body. His T-shirt showed his broad shoulders and lean waist. He had narrow hips and long sinewy veins running down his arms, like rivers on a map. David never wore such tight clothes. She realized suddenly that she had never thought about David's whole body. She had no clear picture of the shape of his chest and where it tapered into his waist. David had been more of a presence. She had never been conscious of his body at all until these last few weeks, and then she had just felt uncomfortable. She had never studied him closely, as she was now studying Jaimie. She blushed as he handed her an ice-cream bar.

"Thanks, Jaimie," she murmured, looking away from him.

"What's the matter? Wrong flavor?"

"No. It's fine. Delicious."

"Where do you go to school?" Jaimie settled against the tree again. His shoulders and arms and hips were so close, Mollie could almost feel them. She edged away, pretending to chase a fly from her legs.

"Springfield. I'll be a freshman."

"How do you feel about college?"

"Feel about it?"

"Yes, do you want to go? Do you like to study?"

"I never really thought about it," Mollie answered slowly. "Everybody I know goes to college, all my friends, my family." She had thought of Springfield only as a place to be on her own, to escape the eye of the family. She had never considered what she wanted to study, or even *if* she wanted to study.

She took a final lick from her ice-cream stick and tried to bury it in the hard ground.

"Trying to plant an ice-cream tree?" Jaimie laughed.

The sound, so close to her ear, made her uneasy. "Thanks for the ice cream. I really must be going."

"Can I walk you somewhere?"

"No, I have to visit my grandmother." But she didn't

59

move. There was something about him she didn't want to leave.

"OK, Little Red Riding Hood. Don't panic. I'm not the wolf." He stretched his mouth wide open. "See, I don't have pointy teeth." No, you have even white teeth that look almost blue, Mollie thought. They were silent for a few minutes, Mollie still digging with her stick.

"Little Red Riding Hood," Mollie said softly. "When I was little, my cousins called me Mollie Make-Believe. We used to play together every Sunday. All of us: Robert and Nate, they're older, and so is Holly. Then there are the younger kids: Holly's twin brothers, Mark and Michael, and my brother, Mayhew." What was she doing, talking to this strange boy? How could he care about the family and those long-ago Sundays?

"What did they do?" He sounded interested.

"Well, we let them play as long as they obeyed us. At first we just kind of ran around. The way we knew the game was over was when some adult called us inside. One day I suggested we play *Caddie Woodlawn*. It was a book I had read that week, about a white settler girl who is stolen by the Indians. Well, anyway, everybody had a part . . ."

"You were Caddie."

"How did you guess?" They both smiled. "After that, every week we played a game with a set plot. I would describe some story and fit each cousin into a part."

"Did they always fit?"

"Sure." She frowned. "No, it didn't always work. One Sunday Robert, the oldest, who's a bookworm, was reading under the willow tree. We couldn't get him to join. So we stretched the story to include an old schoolmaster who sat under a tree all day reading. That was the day Nate called me Mollie Make-Believe. And I guess it stuck." She finished quickly, stunned that she had mentioned Mollie Make-Believe. No one outside the family, not even Hilary, knew her nickname.

"What's in your pack?" she asked quickly.

"A sketch pad and some pencils." He reached for the pack.

All of a sudden Mollie couldn't talk. She had to get away; she nodded to Jaimie and picked up her pocketbook.

"I shall be late," she started.

"Now you sound like the White Rabbit."

She smiled. "Good-bye, Jaimie. I—I enjoyed talking to you."

"Good-bye, Mollie Make-Believe." He looked at her steadily.

"Good-bye, Jaimie."

"Maybe I'll see you here tomorrow," he called as she walked away. She turned back and saw him settling down with his sketch pad. She wouldn't meet him tomorrow. Or ever again.

She crossed to the shady side of the street and walked slowly toward Holly's apartment. She thought of David, but all she saw was Jaimie's arms, arched slightly from his body as he walked. She was disturbed. She was the dependable one; she never talked to strange boys. That was Holly's game. Her parents' disapproving phrases about her cousin were enough to make Mollie look down on Holly's escapades. "Pat and Mike have no sense. Letting her run with that wild crowd. No one can control Holly. Someday they're going to regret giving her all that freedom." Mollie would dissolve

61

if similar remarks were made about her. And yet, even though she never went with "wild boys," she was the one they always seemed to disapprove of. How could she please them? Definitely not by this afternoon. She could never defend Jaimie against the family's raised eyebrows. But Holly wouldn't try to.

"Good afternoon, Miss Mollie. Miss Holly is in her room." Clara's German-soaked English made her sound annoyed. Mollie couldn't tell if the housekeeper believed Holly's sore throat or not.

"Hi, Holly." She could barely distinguish her cousin, a long shadow in the television-lit room. Holly was watching a movie and chewing a sandwich from a half-empty pottery platter.

"Have a seat. Tuna and egg salad here; if you want something else, ask Clara."

"Have you been watching television all day?"

"No, just since I got up." Holly reached to the other side of the chair and handed Mollie a teak bowl filled with potato chips and pretzel sticks. "Have some."

"To look at you, you'd never know Grandmother was sick."

"What do you want me to do, starve myself?" She reached for the remote control and flipped the channel.

Everything Holly did irritated Mollie today. "I just came from the apartment."

"Goody. Is everybody sitting around?"

"What do you expect them to do?" Mollie asked.

"Come off it, Mollie. You act as though you're the only one affected by all this."

"Well, if you're so concerned, why aren't you down there?" Mollie looked at the sandwiches. She was hungry but she didn't want Holly to think she approved of this feast by joining in.

"Did you see Grandmother this morning?" Holly asked, sharply, warning Mollie not to talk about Grandmother unless she wanted a fight.

"We all did." She reached for a sandwich, hoping Holly would take the gesture as a peace offering. "You must have made the egg salad yourself. It's delicious."

"Nobody could eat that crap Clara turns out, with those huge hunks of white."

"And shell in it."

"We had red cabbage for the sixth night last night. I wish Mother would fire her."

"Goddamn Nazi," Mollie said vehemently. She could relax. Holly was in a safe mood. "Your parents mention anything about Grandmother?" Mollie asked.

"Dad's been raging. 'The doctor is incompetent, the nurse is incompetent, the pharmacist is a fool.'" Mollie smiled. Uncle Mike railed against everybody. The newspaperboy didn't fold the paper properly; the carwash missed a spot; the waiter took too long adding up the bill.

"And what about Uncle Rob?" Mollie prompted.

"Well, he was here last night. You know Aunt Cathy never opens her mouth. I think having Robert and Nate and no little girls has permanently stymied her. She just sits, waiting for Uncle Rob. I doubt she's had a thought in ten years." Holly tossed a handful of chips into her mouth.

"I never noticed. But you're right, Hol. I've always thought that she was the same as Mother and Aunt Pat."

"What's the same about them?" Holly said. "Aside from their clothes, they're totally different."

"Mmm, I guess. Somehow I just group them all together."

"I know. Family 6, Mollie 0."

"Have you still been seeing Treacle?" Mollie wanted to change the subject. Holly's irreverent attitude made Mollie feel disloyal, especially when her own parents were Holly's targets.

"Every night. Sunday we went to the Five Spot. He knows more about jazz than Nate ever will." Everybody Holly dated was the best, the smartest, the coolest. But Treacle was a real coup. His father was a British diplomat, and Treacle's sister had gone to a reception with Prince Charles.

Mollie thought about Jaimie. She wanted to tell Holly about him, but she wanted to keep him a secret more. She couldn't stand the thought of Holly making fun of him or teasing her about meeting a boy in the park. And she wasn't sure she could describe him, explain his specialness that had made her so happy.

"I've been thinking, maybe I won't go to Springfield." Mollie was as surprised as Holly. The idea had just come to her.

"What? You've been pushing to get into that place for years. You studied like a maniac."

"Well, if something should happen to Grandmother . . ." She paused, wishing she had never mentioned it.

"Yes?" Holly stared at her.

"Well, Reed will be alone." Yes, that was it. She hated the thought of Reed being alone almost as much as the thought of Grandmother dying. "If I lived with him, he wouldn't be so lonely. I could go to school in New York."

"He's got all his sons, and he can take care of himself. You should go to Springfield and get out from under the family eye."

"They're not so bad, and I would like living with Reed."

"They probably wouldn't let you."

"Forget I mentioned it. And don't say anything to your parents."

"Why should I break a three-year silence on your account?" Holly made a face and clicked the television dial.

Mollie wondered where Jaimie would be next year. She had never felt like talking to a boy as much as she had with Jaimie. She wished he were here now. What would he think of Holly? Those red highlights in his hair. It must be very soft, she thought, smiling to herself.

"What are you smiling so smugly about? Don't tell me you've gotten into some school in New York?"

"Now you're the one who's a little starkers. It was just a thought. Grandmother may be well in a couple of weeks." She wanted to keep Jaimie a secret; she didn't want to share him with anyone.

Chapter Six

"Must you wear those shoes, Mollie?"

"They're the only decent ones I have, Mother." They were driving to Grandmother's. The trip had been reasonably silent; Dad had said nothing. He refused to talk about Grandmother. When Mollie tried to cheer him up, he shook his head irritably, as though she were a mosquito buzzing around his face. Now Mother was starting.

"They look shabby and the heels are run-down."

"Mother, you sound like you're describing a national disaster."

"We'll drop you at Saks. Buy some proper shoes."

"How much should I spend?" Mollie hated to shop. She liked her old clothes; the ones she had grown used to. New ones seemed stiff and foreign.

"Get a simple pair of black shoes. They all cost about the same. John, leave Mollie at Saks." Dad nodded. He had said barely ten words all week.

As the car stopped, Mollie patted her father's head. "Take it easy, Daddy. I'll be there as soon as I can." He looks smaller. I wish he'd storm around like Uncle Mike and Uncle Rob. Then he wouldn't seem so pitiful.

As Mollie went through the revolving door into the perfumed frosted air of the store, Jaimie flashed into her mind. He had said maybe he would see her today. Ridiculous, she thought. In the biggest city in the world, you'll never run into him, if you walk the streets for the next five years. Nevertheless, with a giddy little skip she reversed direction and started walking toward the park. Of course it was silly, but maybe . . . Holly would be astonished if she knew I was searching for a boy in the park, she thought. Family 6, Mollie 0? We'll just see.

Holly did whatever she wanted to. She had probably met countless boys in the park, dated hordes of longhairs. And last year? Reports had drifted back over the family circuit from Vermont, where Holly was studying drama, about weird-looking creatures that Uncle Mike and Aunt Pat had been forced to take to dinner. But somehow Holly always survived the disapproval. She was so sure of herself. Her black hair and eyes emphasized her positiveness. Soon, Mollie reassured herself, she's going to go too far. She's going to bring some freak to Reed's for dinner and maybe then they'll realize how lucky they are to have malleable Mollie.

Ahead the angular glass-and-steel buildings were melting into the soft green of the park. The trees seemed tiny after the huge buildings which had surrounded her. Some people hated the skyscraper walls of the city, but Mollie liked them. They made her feel safe. Her heart was beating faster. What if she saw Jaimie and he didn't recognize her? He couldn't possibly be in the park. He was probably still asleep. Where?

She had no idea where he lived, where he went to school, what his father did. Yet she hadn't stopped thinking about him since she had left him yesterday. If only she could talk to David the way she rambled on to Jaimie. Because she knew where David was.

She paused as she crossed the street into the park. Would he think she had deliberately come to the park to see him? She could say that she was taking a walk before visiting Grandmother. And act wide-eyed with surprise to see him. It would not be hard since it would be more magic than coincidence to run into him when she wanted to so much.

"Hi, Mollie." She stumbled as she heard her name. A long tanned arm reached out and caught her; pale blond hairs on the arm. She looked up, stunned.

"You could say hello." Jaimie grinned. "Or if you don't want to say hello, sit down. Since you insist on wearing fancy dresses, you'd better try the bench."

"Jaimie." She couldn't think of anything to say.

"That's a good sign. You recognize me."

"I'm on my way to Grandmother's. I thought I'd take a walk."

"This is where I came in." He laughed and stretched his legs out in front of him.

"Where's your pack, your sketch pad?"

"I didn't come up here to sketch; I came to look for you."

"With all the people in New York, Jaimie, you could walk the streets for five years and not run into me." She hoped he didn't notice her face was turning red.

"Except that I did. On the first try too. How come you're going to see your grandmother? Didn't you visit her yesterday?"

"Yes. But she's sick. The whole family goes every day."

"How awful."

"Yes, she's—" Mollie stopped. She shouldn't discuss Grandmother's illness with him.

"I mean how awful to be around sickness every day. It must be a real bummer."

"Not really." She thought for a minute. "I mean we all go, and, well, I don't mind.'

"I would."

"But you'd visit your grandmother if she were sick, wouldn't you?"

"Unless she had something contagious." They laughed. He was so silly. Mollie wanted to hug him. She quickly put her arms behind her and clutched the slats of the bench. Jaimie was looking at her. She gripped the cold metal harder, but she was still smiling.

"Are all your cousins there every day?"

She nodded, pleased that he was interested. "If anything happens, I mean if my grandmother dies, I think I'll go to school in New York and live with my grandfather." She sighed and loosened her grip on the bench.

"I don't see the connection." He hung his head backward over the bench, and Mollie stared at his broad chest. It seemed familiar today; also his flat stomach and narrow hips.

"I'll live with him." She swung her feet under the bench to hide her shoes. "Then he won't be alone."

"Instead of Springfield? You're crazy."

"My cousin Holly said that too. It's just an idea. I'll probably end up at Springfield."

"What do *you* want to do?" He was looking at her again. She felt his breath on her cheek.

"I don't know. Everything is confused. Grandmother just

got sick. I haven't talked to my grandfather or to my parents." He was still looking at her. She stood up to go. Jaimie's hand reached out. She was back on the bench.

"I've got to go, Jaimie."

"I know. You have to go to your grandmother's, Little Red."

"I do."

"You're unique, Mollie." He shook his head. "Most girls would be flattered if I came up to the park early in the morning on the million-to-one shot of running into them. You on the other hand . . ."

"I am flattered, Jaimie. I'm glad to see you. It's just, well, I don't know you," she finished in a whisper.

"A good way to remedy that is to have coffee with me."

"But my grandmother." There was a coffee shop a block from Grandmother's. Maybe . . . she didn't want to leave him. She blinked as she caught Jaimie's eye. "There's a coffee shop near Grandmother's."

Jaimie took her hand as they crossed the street and didn't let it go as they continued walking. I've held hands with dozens of boys, Mollie thought. I shouldn't feel this way.

In the coffee shop Mollie piled up two stacks of sugar packets, aligning their corners. Just an ordinary coffee shop, drinking an ordinary cup of coffee with an ordinary boy, she thought, trying to steady herself.

"Want some cake or pie?" Jaimie motioned toward the row of clear-domed containers that covered crumbling wedges of devil's food cake and coconut custard pie.

"Just coffee, thanks."

She leaned her chin on her clasped hands and tried to weed through the myriad of questions in her mind. There was so much she wanted to know about Jaimie. She bent her head and fiddled with the sugar packets, hoping he hadn't noticed her staring at him.

"Are you going to be a painter?"

"It's hard to say. I like to paint, but at the moment I'm more involved in crafts—making jewelry, furniture, collages. Especially weaving cloth."

"You don't seem craftsy. You know, the leather-and-silver-belt type."

He leaned toward her and half closed his eyes. "You've got to create your own things in order to realize how many things there are to create. In our society everything is ready-made, already finished for us. Unless we play the process backwards and get involved in the actual creation, we are losing an essential communication with ourselves."

"What do you mean, 'essential communication with ourselves'?" Ordinarily she would have smiled and pretended to understand, but she had to really understand and remember everything he was saying.

He took a sip of coffee and continued, "You eat bread every day, right? But have you ever made a loaf yourself?"

"As a matter of fact, I have."

"Well?" He was so serious. She had never had real talks with David. She knew little about him, even though she had been dating him for almost a year. She knew what kind of movies he liked, who his friends were—all information. A collection of facts about David, but no feelings. Jaimie was looking at her expectantly.

"It smelled marvelous while it was baking." Mollie wished she understood Jaimie's point so she could say the perfect thing.

"While you were eating it, weren't you conscious of its taste and smell and texture? Instead of just swallowing it, like we swallow that rubbery white bread from the supermarket?"

"You're right." She kept nodding and stirring her coffee, picturing rows of spongy tasteless loaves of bread; she could almost feel them clogging her throat. "I've never thought about the bread I usually eat." She swallowed heavily. "But you're right. I do remember, even now, the loaf of bread I baked. You eat store-bread automatically."

"And you wear clothes automatically too. But if you decorate a shirt, or weave your own cloth, you're really in contact with it. You've made it your own. If you buy something finished, it never belongs to you in the same way."

Jaimie stretched out his arm, and Mollie took his hand.

Mollie wanted to touch his hair. "There's none of you in it." She paused, suddenly aware that they were holding hands in a coffee shop in the middle of the morning. "It could belong to anyone. I guess I've never put myself into anything." She felt hollow; she held Jaimie's hand tighter as though to protect herself from disappearing.

"I'll teach you to weave if you want." He touched her cheek. I'll never forget this moment, she thought. If I hadn't wandered into the park yesterday, I would never have met him. It was a sign.

"Where do you live, Jaimie?"

"In a loft downtown, near the Battery."

"A loft?"

"Yeah. It looks like an airplane hangar that a band of gypsies deserted in the middle of a celebration."

"What about your parents?"

"They live in South Carolina."

"Are they furious about you living here?"

"Not at all. Mom's a textile designer. She taught me to weave. But I was coming North to school and I decided to stay. There's nothing to do at home except hang around a country club in the summer."

Mollie looked down at her empty cup. How he would hate her friends and their indolent summers. She was suddenly embarrassed for filling her days with dumb movies and David. She looked at Jaimie. "I would love to learn to weave, to make something that is only mine," she said.

"You can, Mollie Make-Believe."

"I do have to get to my grandmother's," she said regretfully, looking at him sadly. "It's getting late."

"Same time, same bench tomorrow, Little Red?"

"Same time, same bench, Mr. Wolf." They smiled at each other, and Mollie didn't stop smiling all the way to Grandmother's. She could barely contain her excitement as she rang the bell.

"Good morning, dear. Don't you look nice."

Mollie asked Reed about Grandmother, hoping in the dimly lit hallway he wouldn't notice how happy she looked.

"She's a little tired today. The doctor will be here in about an hour."

"That's good, Reed." Mollie walked into the living room.

"Hello, Mother, Aunt Cathy." Mother looked at her.

"Let me see the shoes," Mother said. She reached for a new strand of wool for her needlepoint.

"Shoes?" Mollie stopped short. "Yes, shoes. Well, Mother, they didn't have any that fit me. That's what took so long. Anyway, I'm considering making my own shoes. Has there

73

ever been a cobbler in the family?" She was so keyed up, such a large part of her was still in the coffee shop with Jaimie, that she felt insulated against her mother's reaction.

"This is neither the time nor the place for your nonsense." Mother looked up and said sharply, "Where are the shoes?"

"All safely nestled in their ready-made boxes, waiting for ignorant people to buy them."

"What do you mean, ignorant people?"

"Mother, let sleeping shoes sleep." She smiled, walked toward Nate, who was standing at the window, and thought, Family 6, Mollie 6.

Chapter Seven

"Let's go to the Happyburger on Lexington," Holly said as she and Mollie and Nate slipped quietly from the apartment. They were going out for lunch because too many people in the apartment would cause confusion, especially with the doctor expected any minute. Mother and Aunt Cathy and Aunt Pat made a great effort to have the apartment pin-straight neat before the doctor arrived. Everyone appeared calm, steady—as though each of them had to convince the doctor of her skill in dealing with illness.

Yesterday when the doorman had announced the doctor's arrival, Reed had hastily reached for his suit jacket and neatly arranged his white handkerchief in his breast pocket before opening the door. Robert greeted the doctor by asking him a question about the newest procedure in interpreting data from enzyme tests. Mollie and Nate had looked at each other in surprise, and watched as Robert seemed to move out of the family circle and into a conspiratorial role with the doctor.

After the doctor had examined Grandmother, he spoke to Reed and Reed's sons. Robert joined them, and later he expanded on the doctor's meager responses, answering his mother's questions in a dispassionate, logical tone. "If he gives her any more opiates, her symptoms will be masked, and he won't be able to determine whether the treatment is successful."

When the adults drifted into the library, Mollie turned to Robert and said, "It's Grandmother you're talking about, not some guinea pig."

"What's wrong with her anyway?" Holly asked casually. They waited tensely.

"I don't know."

"You're a stinking liar," Holly said calmly.

"Please tell us, Robert," Mollie asked, hoping he wouldn't. It was better to think Grandmother would be getting well soon, thinking of her illness as some vague mystery. If Robert gave them too many details, it might not be possible to pretend any longer.

He muttered something indistinguishable and reached for his book. No! He's breaking us up again, just like when he outgrew the playhouse, Mollie thought unhappily. She reached out for Nate's arm and winked at Holly. "Let's leave Young Dr. Snotnose and get some ice cream, the three of us." They had to stay together.

"Mollie," Nate said, shaking her by the arm. "What about the Happyburger?"

"It's too plastic," Mollie said, wishing Jaimie could hear her.

"It's too what?" Nate looked at her.

"Nate, do you really taste what you eat? Think of the

76

thousands of impersonal cheeseburgers you have eaten."

"Why should I?" asked Nate.

"Could you explain this world-beating question over some food at the Happyburger?" Holly punched the elevator button several times. "After lunch I'll let you know what I tasted. OK?"

"Don't twist my words. You always do that. Anyway, I was talking to Nate." She always loses patience with me when I try to start a discussion, Mollie thought. She's only nice when I'm asking her advice or when I don't know how to handle something.

"Nate is hungry, and Nate can't answer questions on an empty stomach," he said pulling both his cousins into the elevator.

"Bloody diplomat," muttered Holly, but Mollie was glad they were all walking together cheerfully, like the musketeers of their childhood. She looked at both of them fondly.

"Holly, remember how we used to bite the doctor when he gave us shots?"

"I remember the two of you practically running every pediatrician out of town." They laughed together and Mollie felt secure. She loved them all, even Robert.

They walked down the tree-shaded street for a few minutes, in silence. This neighborhood was a deserted movie set. No children bounced balls against the building walls, or unscrewed the fire hydrants on hot days; no people gathered on stoops at dusk. There were no stoops, only carpeted hallways guarded by doormen dressed in uniforms that blended with the canopies above them.

"Without the taxi horns and people pushing past each other, this town is almost possible," Nate said.

"Don't you like the city?" asked Mollie.

"Most of the time I guess I'm inured to the noise and crowds. But after being in the country, I realize how rarely I see the sky in this place."

"Walt Whitman," Holly singsonged. How can I get her out of this mood, Mollie thought quickly, so we can all be like we used to be? But Holly continued, "What do you want to do, Nate, live in Walden Pond?"

"Not *in* it," Nate answered mildly.

"Where else can you see every single movie the instant it opens, and all the concerts and ballets and museums?"

Damn her. "When was the last time you went to a museum?" Mollie asked angrily, preparing herself for Holly's hot annoyance.

"Don't twist my words. You always do that."

"OK, you two, let's not hassle." Nate the mediator. He opened the door to the Happyburger and Mollie mouthed a "thank you" to him behind Holly's back.

"C'mon, Nate, do your Harvardian I-demand-a-table bit." Holly turned to Mollie. "I can't wait to see you taste your food." Is she always this sarcastic, Mollie wondered. She felt as though there were a stranger sitting up in her head, commenting on Holly.

After they gave the waiter their order, Nate smiled. "Now, what were you saying about tasting food?" He was using his teasing tone, the one she had first heard when he nicknamed her Mollie Make-Believe.

If she could explain it as well as Jaimie had, they would be as amazed at the concept as she had been. And then, maybe, she could tell them about Jaimie. Just like in the old days, a secret would bind them together. She looked up expectantly, anxious for their reactions, anticipating their interest.

78

"Everything we do, like eating processed food and wearing completely store-bought clothes, it's all done for us. I mean, we don't have any part in it, none of ourselves is in it. I mean it's not really *ours*." The words tumbled out.

"Would you run through that one more time, kid? So far it's not terrifically clear." Nate leaned back in his chair, balancing on the two back legs. Mollie clenched her teeth. They were so stupid, so sure of themselves. Thank God she had met Jaimie. Thank God she had not told them about him. She could communicate with a boy she had met only twenty-four hours ago and her cousins, whom she had known all her life, were as dense as the rest of the family. She snatched up her cheeseburger and concentrated on every juicy bite. And she resolutely tuned out Holly and Nate's voices.

She would see Jaimie tomorrow, no matter what. Jaimie, slouched down on the park bench, his legs slanting out before him and his arms resting along the back of the bench. If only she were in the park with him now. She touched her palm, feeling his warm, slightly calloused hand around hers. Nate and Holly probably thought she was sulking, but they could never guess she was thinking of the way Jaimie's hazel eyes caught yellow fish-quick glints in certain lights.

Nate glanced at his watch and tossed his crumpled napkin onto his plate. "We'd better get back. We've been gone almost two hours."

"I think I'll go home and nap." Holly pushed some hair off her neck with the back of her hand.

"Still feeling sickly, Cuz?" Mollie's concern was mostly sarcasm, a tone she rarely attempted around experts.

Holly glared at Mollie. Not any more, that newly born commentator in Mollie's head declared. She's not fooling me anymore. And if I've figured her out, Reed is bound to. Later he'll remember how she ditched the family, running home when Grandmother was sick and she should have been there.

"I don't like sitting in that tomb, with icy air blowing on my neck, and everybody waiting around for Grandmother to die." Holly got up, shoved back the table, and walked quickly to the door, holding her pocketbook in front of her to clear a path. Mollie gasped and looked at Nate. But he didn't say a word. Just reached into his pocket, threw some change onto the table, and motioned her to follow him.

They left the restaurant and found Holly tapping her foot at the corner. "How could you say that?" Mollie asked her, as though there had been no pause in the conversation.

"I suppose you enjoy sitting there every day?"

"Nobody likes it, obviously. But it's something you have to do."

"Why?"

"Holly, you know why as well as I do," she said.

"I love Grandmother as much as anyone, but I won't watch her die." Holly turned and walked away, disappearing into the sidewalk crush of people.

"You have to," Mollie called after her, her hands clenched so that Nate would not see that she was trembling all over.

They walked down the block. When Nate didn't say anything, she turned to him. "She's so selfish. Wow. Grandmother is sick, Reed is so upset, and all she can do is think of her own selfish self."

"Listen, Mollie, you can stay home too. Nobody's forcing you to hang around the apartment every day." Stay home? She would never be able to face Reed if she avoided being

80

there now. Holly might be able to, but Mollie couldn't. Didn't Nate see that?

"I'm not deserting the family," Mollie said. Nate widened his eyes and glanced at her sideways. She caught his look and her anger disappeared. "How do you think we'll remember her?" she said.

"Like Grandmother. The Christmas parties, her laugh, our fathers' respect for her. I guess we'll each have our own memories."

"Do you think we'll remember her pale, without any strength? Every day when I go in there, I'm afraid that's the only part I'll remember." She stopped as her voice became a squeak.

"I don't know, Moll. I never knew anyone who died."

"And Reed. Nate, when I was walking up to the apartment this morning, I saw this old man, and he was sitting in a wrinkled shirt in the park reading the newspaper all alone."

"Stop it. Reed's got all of us—"

"But what if he changes without Grandmother?"

Nate laughed and gave her shoulder a squeeze. "C'mon, little cousin, Reed is not going to wear wrinkled shirts in the park. And besides he has the paper delivered."

Mollie turned on him. "Can't you ever be serious?"

"It won't help. There's nothing we can do," he said sadly.

"Well, there's something *I* can do," Mollie said firmly. "I am going to live with him, and he won't be alone."

"What are you talking about?"

"I'm going to live with Reed and stay in New York. Then he won't be alone."

"You can't take Grandmother's place, Mollie."

"Of course I can't. But at least he won't be alone."

"When you get to Springfield, I'll show you around Cambridge. You'll love it, Mollie."

"I'm not kidding, Nate. I'm going to stay with Reed if they let me. I won't go to Springfield."

"OK." He guided her beneath the gold-and-white canopy into the building. "But in the likely event that you turn up in Cambridge this fall, I promise to show you around. And Holly will surely appear for a few football games. We Fieldses will tear up the town." It was impossible to stay angry at Nate, and he did paint a great picture of Cambridge. They probably wouldn't let her stay with Reed anyway. And Grandmother might recover.

"You're right, Nate." Mollie smiled.

"I was nervous before I went to Harvard, you know."

"You, the most dashing young man in the East?"

"Deep down, Mollie, I'm just plain folks, but don't let anyone find out."

Chapter Eight

Driving home with Mother, Dad having left earlier to attend a crucial meeting at the office, Mollie tried to develop an airtight plan for meeting Jaimie the next day. Mother drove fast, refused to have the car radio on, and rarely talked. About halfway home Mollie apologized for not having bought shoes that morning.

"I was looking at stacks and stacks of shoes, and then I started to think about Grandmother." Mollie's stomach knotted at this embellishment. It would serve me right if she died while I'm talking, she thought.

"Well, anyway, Mother," she said recovering quickly, "I wanted to get up to the apartment, and you know how those salesmen want to cram the most expensive ones down your throat. . . ."

"But you should have forced yourself to decide upon a pair of shoes. It wouldn't have taken you any longer. You'll have to learn to figure things out for yourself. I won't be at Springfield to tell you when to buy shoes, and what shoes to buy."

"If you drop me off tomorrow morning, I'll snap up a pair in a jiffy. Really nice ones. I'm sorry I messed up today."

"You don't have to go in tomorrow, Mollie. Stay home and charge the shoes at Maxwell's." She moved her foot to the brake, clicked out two quarters from the ice-cream-man change holder Dad had mounted on the dashboard. She smiled at the toll man. She could stop in the middle of a scream, and after she buzzed the electric car window closed, continue it on the same note. No time for idle thoughts, Mollie reminded herself; I have to see Jaimie tomorrow.

"I want to go in tomorrow, Mom. Then if Grandmother seems stronger, I can stay home for the weekend."

"You can't wear those shoes, Mollie."

"I can wear them one more day. Grandmother is more important than my scuffy shoes."

"Your grandmother would be horrified to see those shoes."

"I'll stand very close to her bed, where she won't be able to see my feet." Mollie laughed, but her mother's head drooped slightly. "I'm sorry, Mom. That wasn't in very good taste."

"Maybe we can all stay home this weekend," Mother sighed. Mollie looked at her closely. She seemed tired; her makeup was worn off; she hadn't done her usual touch-up before leaving Reed's. It hadn't occurred to Mollie that Mother might not relish these long days, tiptoeing around and waiting to be useful.

"When will Dad get home?"

"I don't know. But as soon as he does, we're all going out to dinner. Running into town every day has destroyed my schedule. There's nothing left in the freezer. I haven't had a minute to get to the market, and I'm too tired to cook tonight." Poor Mother. It was getting to her. I prefer her this way, Mollie thought. She seems more like a person than an emissary from *House Beautiful*.

"I'll shop over the weekend, if you want."

"That would be a help, dear." She sighed again. "We probably won't get to the Cape this summer the way things look."

"Does that mean Grandmother is getting better or worse?"

"I don't know. Why don't you ask your Aunt Pat? She seems privy to all the inside information." Mollie was surprised by the edge of bitterness in her mother's voice. Then her thoughts went back to Jaimie.

"Why don't you ever bake bread, Mom?"

"I have enough to do taking care of all of you." Mother's voice had returned to normal; her body regained its usual starch.

"Could I bake some this weekend?"

Mother didn't answer and they returned to silence, Mollie thinking about Jaimie. Would he really teach her to weave? What kind of cloth would she make? She couldn't imagine designing her own patterns. There's probably some trick to it, she decided. He'll know all about it. I'll wear that green dress tomorrow; if only I could do something to it, make it more mine before I see Jaimie, so that he would know I understand.

"Mom, will you teach me to embroider?"

"Certainly, dear. When things settle down a bit."

85

"What about tonight? I want to embroider some flowers on my green dress."

"You are not going to ruin that good dress with flowers."

"Mother, it's my dress."

"Mollie, if you want to learn embroidery, you will start on some old scraps."

"Mother, that green dress is the same as any other green dress."

"And it's going to remain that way." Damn. Just when Mollie thought she was being nice, Mother set up roadblocks. She was ruining everything. Jaimie would have loved some blue flowers, looking as though they had grown right out of the grass-green dress. Mollie leaned against the door, as far away from her mother as she could get.

As Mother eased the car into the garage, Mayhew came out of the house. "Hi, Mom. How's Grandmother?"

"A little better today, dear." He looked at Mollie, who nodded in confirmation. She felt privileged to have the information firsthand. She hated looking at Grandmother lying so limp in that bed and she hated the hooded silence in the apartment all day, but at least she was allowed to go.

"Can't I go tomorrow? Please, Mom. I'll be quiet and won't bother anyone." Mayhew followed his mother into the house. He said the same thing every day and Mollie knew what Mother's answer would be. Instead of listening, she wandered toward the willow grove.

Jaimie was going to teach her to weave; she would have her own cloth. Would her parents let her get a loom? She wondered if Jaimie would consider cutting his hair just a little to meet the family. Holly would be no ally—she was super-conventional now that she was attending diplomatic receptions with Treacle. There was a sliver of a chance that

86

Dad might understand. He didn't make bread or weave, God knows, but he fiddled with all those things in his lab and he constantly made improvements on the television set, the stereo, and other machinery. That was changing finished things, modifying them into his own personal equipment. They had the best television reception of anyone she knew. It could be considered the same if only Daddy would see it that way. She looked up. Mayhew was walking toward her, his lower lip thrust out.

"Hi, kid," she said, ignoring his tragic look. "Have a piece of ground. It's free."

He sat down and shook his head viciously. "They treat me like a baby. Why do I have to stay home, while everybody else gets to see Grandmother?"

"The twins aren't there."

"I'm two years older than they are. They're still going to camp, for God's sake."

"Don't get mad at me. I don't care if you go in there every day. You can sleep at the foot of Grandmother's bed for all of me."

"Can't you talk to them, Moll? I hate being stuck at home."

"They won't listen to me."

"Won't you talk to Reed?" he pleaded.

"Talk to him yourself. He's your grandfather too." She was pleased that Hew had asked her to intercede with Reed. He knew she might have a chance where he would not. "OK, if the opportunity presents itself. Some days he's too upset about Grandmother to talk."

"Please? Tomorrow?" He looked so forlorn. She felt sorry for him. She nodded and smiled at him.

She really should protect him; he was alone. "I'll talk to

Reed tomorrow. It's not that they don't want you around. They just want to spare you."

"Spare me from what?"

"It's pretty depressing. Whispering around the apartment and having to act cheerful even though Grandmother sleeps most of the time."

"Are you depressed?"

"Yes."

"You don't seem depressed. You're nicer today than you've been in months. You were a real bitch the last two weeks." That was before Jaimie, she thought. "What are you smiling about? You really have been impossible."

"Let's just say I'm coping better. I've adjusted. You may not be able to do that. You're not as old as I am," she finished.

"You're getting snotty again."

"Do you ever taste the bread you eat, Hew? I mean *taste* it?"

"I know what taste means. Of course I do, I'm not a complete moron."

"No, think about it carefully. Are you conscious of the bread you eat?"

"If I were unconscious, I wouldn't be able to chew." Hew started to giggle uncontrollably.

"You're so thick it's like talking to a tree." She got up and walked toward the house. They were all impossible. She did not belong in this family.

Hew stopped laughing and ran after her. "I didn't mean it. I was just teasing. Please ask Reed tomorrow."

"I said I would."

"Thanks, Moll. And I'll start concentrating on my bread,

saltines, melba toast, anything you say." He laughed again.

"Can't you do something about that laugh? It makes you sound dumber than you are—and that's not easy." She slammed the door, annoyed that she had let him get to her.

As she closed the car door the following morning, Mollie thought, "Only twenty-four hours since I got out of the car at precisely the same place. And yet I am completely changed. I can't wait to see Jaimie." She felt guilty about her high spirits. As she was falling asleep last night she pictured Grandmother tossing in her bed, the night barely distinguishable from the day. But nothing would smash the joy Mollie felt about Jaimie. With her arms wrapped snugly around her pillow she had smiled late into the night.

Now she waited until her parents had driven out of sight, then vigorously circled through the revolving door. I'll *have* to buy some shoes, she reminded herself. But she had no time to think about them now. She hurried uptown, straining toward the park. I'd better slow down. I don't want to get there panting and sweaty. She forced herself to slow down, pausing every few minutes to count all the items in a store window. As she saw the green of the park she smoothed her hair, looked at her reflection in a window, and headed for their bench. She was going to a special bench, not idly strolling across the cobblestones like all these other people. She waved to the hot-dog man standing beside his blue-and-yellow umbrella-shaded wagon, wanting to tell him, "I'm going to meet the most incredible boy. He's going to teach me to weave."

He was there, sitting on the bench, legs stretched out in

front of him, wearing a white T-shirt with some writing on it. Mollie couldn't see it clearly.

"Hi, Jaimie." She hoped she sounded calm. She didn't want him to guess that thoughts of him had blocked out practically everything else since she had met him.

"Hi, there." The shirt said "Staten Island Ferry" in archaic red script. A blue-and-red ferry was silhouetted against the New York skyline. Faded to the perfect shade.

"Jaimie, what a superb shirt! I love it." She shook her head in wonder. She felt so plain next to him.

"Clever of you to wear a green dress. You'll blend in with the park. Let's walk."

"Don't let me blend too far—so that I look like one of the trees to you." He reached for her hand.

They walked down a slope studded with uniformed nurses and small children clumsily rolling rubber balls close to their carriages, a few couples lying on their backs to catch the sun on their faces, and an occasional solitary individual bent over a book.

Mollie squeezed Jaimie's hand. "What a super-glorious day."

"You seem so happy, Mollie. Is your grandmother better?" Mollie frowned. What a beast she was. Laughing and strolling through the park with Jaimie while Grandmother was lying against that mass of pillows in that bed.

"A little," Mollie answered. She shouldn't be here.

If Jaimie hadn't mentioned Grandmother, Mollie wouldn't have thought about her at all.

"Let's go to the zoo." He tugged at her hand and led her up the hill toward the seal pond. Hundreds of times Grandmother had taken her and Holly to see the seals!

"Actually, Jaimie, I shouldn't . . ."

"Your grandmother, right?" He didn't laugh at her or try to talk her out of leaving.

"Yes," she said reluctantly. She had to talk to Reed about Hew and it was wrong to stay. The longer she was with Jaimie, the less she wanted to leave.

"Well, we can leave the park through the zoo."

"Great idea."

"You have the quickest mood changes, Mollie Make-Believe. What is it? Do you want to talk about it?"

"No, Jaimie; it's nothing." She didn't want to spoil their day. He nodded. "OK," he said. He never pushes me; he seems content with whatever I say, she thought. The sun was glowing behind him. Those red highlights in his hair. She stopped, abruptly, her eyes searching his face. Jaimie bent down and kissed her. When he started to pull away, she reached up and kissed him. She didn't want it to stop. As they gradually moved apart, she realized they were standing in the middle of the park, with thousands of people around. She had stopped thinking completely. She couldn't remember what they had been talking about. She looked at Jaimie quickly and smiled shyly. She should leave. But this is one "should" I'm going to ignore, she thought.

"C'mon, Jaimie. The seals are my favorites. Especially the old one who points his nose in the air and barks at the crowd. He's a total ham."

There was a big crowd gathered at the pond. They had to twist their way through a tangle of children to find a clear place at the rail. "It's easier to push little kids around," Jaimie whispered.

"You're a bully," she whispered back, liking the closeness of talking into his ear, his hair tickling her nose.

"Let's go to the polar bears. They're the best."

"The polar bears? You can never see them. They're always inside that phony cave."

"But, dear Little Red, have you ever climbed to the top of the rocks behind the cave?"

"No, never even thought of it." How often had he come to the park before she had met him?

"It takes someone from South Carolina to come North and point the way to you dumb Yankees," he drawled.

"How come you don't sound like South Carolina?" she asked. She hadn't thought of his speech as southern. She loved to hear him pronounce her name, emphasizing the first syllable. She would never again think of it any other way. *Mol*lie. "I can't describe it, but you know what I mean."

"There are as many southern accents as there are northern, Missy," he said in a high-pitched drawl.

"I didn't mean southern accents are bad, Jaimie."

"Didn't say you did, honeychile. Why we have as many speech variations down home, sugar, as there were rebel soldiers in *Gone With the Wind*."

"OK, I get the point, Rhett."

"Now we go down this here path, and then up that there hill."

"C'mon, stop talking like that." She laughed.

"Maybe this field trip isn't such a terrific idea. You'll get filthy."

"I don't care. Now that I know it's there, I've got to see the back of the bear cave." She smiled at him. "These shoes are headed for the trash anyway."

"What's your family like?" he asked, as they climbed toward the smooth gray rocks.

"My grandfather is fantastic. He and I are very close. We

92

have a large family and spend lots of time together." She paused. How could she explain her family? "They're the same as any other family."

"All families are just individuals sharing a common name."

"Don't you like your family?"

"Certainly. I like some of them and don't like others. You know, like the soldiers—"

"In *Gone With the Wind*." They finished together.

"Now give me your hand, and wedge your right foot on that root, and kind of fall toward that bluish rock. Don't be afraid. I'll catch you."

She looked down. Jaimie had climbed up so easily; she would look like a fool if she slipped. She tried to move her right foot but it wouldn't budge. "Jaimie, can't we do this another way?"

"Don't be afraid, Mollie. I promise, you won't get hurt." She was once more standing in the outfield, with the strongest girl at bat. She didn't want Jaimie to know she couldn't handle the rocks, but she didn't want him to see her clumsiness either.

"Jaimie, let's do it another day. I've got to get to my grandmother's. It's lunchtime, and I should have been there an hour ago; maybe next week?" It was no good. He knew she was afraid.

"Mollie, I've got your hand and I promise you won't fall."

She took a deep breath, clutched his hand, wedged her foot into the space between the root and the rock, and gasped as she fell. A split second later she was safely on the rock with Jaimie's arms around her. "Now where are these famous bears?" Could he feel her trembling?

"I didn't say you'd see the bears. Just the back of the cave. Be patient." He lay against the sun-warmed rock and Mollie smoothed her skirt and lay back too. The hardness of the stone felt secure under her head. The tenseness drained from her legs. She turned to Jaimie, who was talking steadily.

"My father owns a small mill. He wants me to work for him. Same old cliché. Father and son."

"You wouldn't work in a mill," she said positively. It was impossible to imagine him surrounded by noisy machines and grubby millhands.

"I may."

"Be serious."

"I am. I don't know what I'll do. My father is not a bad guy. And the day may come when running a mill appeals to me."

"I thought you said you were an artist. What about weaving cloth and making your own bread?" she said.

"They weave cloth in *mills*, my dear." He laughed and pinched her nose.

"But Jaimie—" She couldn't finish the sentence.

"I didn't say I *was* going to run the mill. I just said I might. I also might cut my hair and become an astronaut."

"They don't have brown-eyed astronauts." She poked his stomach lightly. He had only been kidding. Making conversation.

"Well, then I won't be an astronaut. A bear?" He sat up and looked at her. "I'll be the resident park bear. And never come out of my cave."

As he leaned down to kiss her, Mollie smiled. This was the most perfect day of her life. She had found the one person who would understand everything. Was that how Hilary felt about Eddie? Was that why she had kept him a secret from Mollie?

"What will you be doing in the fall?" she said, touching Jaimie's arm.

"Not sure yet. Maybe go back to school. Maybe Europe."

"What school?"

"I went to Harvard," he said flatly.

"You went to Harvard! My cousin Nate Fields is a junior. You know him? Tall, reddish hair?" She would never have guessed Jaimie went to Harvard. Grandmother would be pleased. Mollie sighed. Grandmother. It was time to leave.

"I didn't know too many guys."

"How many years did you go?"

"One. I'm thinking of going to Europe and then back to Harvard. Maybe it won't seem like so much of a grind then."

"Why go back at all? You can be an artist without Harvard."

"Except that I don't know what I want to do." Mollie was confused. He had said he *was* an artist, and now he was saying he didn't know. Nate and Robert had known for years what they were going to be. David wasn't sure what he would become, but he didn't have any talent—anything special. He would do whatever came along when he graduated. But at least he knew that much.

"Jaimie, you said you were an artist. Why not go to art school?"

"Because an artist's vision is more important than his technique. And the vision quotient at Harvard is higher than at some sketching class—at least for me right now. I can always take painting courses later. I'm not going to dry up like a tube of old paint."

He seemed unconcerned with making a decision. Grandmother would not like that. She sat up and looked down toward the small pond where the bears were supposed to be. "Still no bears, my friend."

"I never promised you a rose garden." He laughed and stood up. He looked at the sky, stretched, and walked to the edge of the rock.

"I didn't ask for a rose garden—just bears."

"C'mon, Little Red, I'll walk you to the edge of the park." She hated to leave him. She had a feeling that it would never again be the same. There had been a special magic up here, their secret bear cave. "What are you doing this weekend?" he said as they were climbing down the rocks.

It's a lot easier going down this thing than climbing up, she thought thankfully. "Nothing. Maybe visit Grandmother. Depends on my parents."

"Want to come down to the loft?"

She could see all Jaimie's things—his loom, his paintings, his whole life! It would be like getting inside his head. Better even than the bear cave.

"I don't see how I can, but I'll try."

They were standing outside the park, near the vendors. "Here's my phone number. Call me tonight if you can, and we'll make plans." He touched her chin and kissed her nose. "Would you like an ice cream?"

"Toasted almond, please." As he walked toward the ice-cream man, Mollie knew how he looked. She knew how he walked, how he smiled without opening his mouth, she could remember the exact color of his teeth, the shape of his hands, those veins on his arms. She loved their secrets—ice-cream trees, the bear cave, Little Red. As he walked toward her, she couldn't wait for him to move through the crowd around the balloon vendor. She ran toward him and squeezed his hand—knowing without looking that the Staten Island Ferry was a beautiful faded red.

Chapter Nine

Mollie hesitated in front of the door of her grandparents' apartment. Inside she was bubbling and jumping. Not the way to feel for visiting Grandmother. Think about Grandmother. She might die. She might die. Mollie repeated it over and over but they were just words. Jaimie's loft. I'm going to Jaimie's loft. The thought made goosebumps on her arms.

She rang the doorbell. Mother opened the door. "Where have you been? We've been worried about you. You seem flushed."

"I was climbing the bear cave with a boy."

Mother grabbed her arm and pulled her into the library. "Listen to me, young lady, this is no time for your wisecracks. Your grandmother is very ill, very ill," Mother repeated, "and we have enough problems without you creating more. Now where have you been?" Mollie had never noticed the tiny wrinkles patterning her mother's face. Not deep wrinkles; a light layer of cobwebs, as though someone forgot to dust her, Mollie thought.

"Mollie, if you don't tell me where you've been, you will have your father to contend with." She paused and looked down at Mollie's feet. "I don't believe it. You didn't buy shoes!" Mother's voice was a hushed scream.

"What's going on in here?" Father was standing in the doorway, somber in his dark gray suit. For the first time Mollie saw the deep indentations under his eyelids. They made his cheeks appear fuller than they actually were. "Where have you been, Mollie?"

She felt sorry for him. She said softly, "I went to the park. I walked around the zoo and tried to forget about Grandmother." Her legs went weak. She felt as though she were betraying both Grandmother and Jaimie.

"Let it go, Cyn. The doctor will be leaving in a few minutes, and I want to hear what he has to say." This must be awful for him, Mollie thought. He can always fix his machines, but here there's nothing he can do.

She followed him into the living room. Uncle Rob was standing closest to Reed. The eldest son. King Arthur's squire accompanying him into battle.

"Be quiet in there." Mother's whisper followed her. "Remember the doctor is here."

Holly was on the couch with her unending supply of magazines spread out around her.

"Where's your mother?" Mollie mouthed as she sat down next to her.

"Doing errands. She decided there were a few things Grandmother wants."

"You caused quite a stir this morning," Nate said, balancing on the arm of the couch.

"Can't be perfect all the time," Mollie answered.

Holly was studying her. "You look quite good today, Moll."

"Thanks, Cuz." Mollie motioned Holly toward the kitchen. She hadn't decided how to ask her, but she needed her cousin's help to arrange this weekend in New York. Especially with Mother fired up about the shoes.

"What is with you this morning?" Holly frowned. "You've got to get rid of that silly grin."

"I need your help." She looked steadily at her cousin.

"What did you do, knock over Tiffany's?"

"I want to spend the weekend at your house."

"What's the big drama? We have plenty of room. The twins left this morning."

"My parents will wonder why I want to stay. They'll want me to go home with them."

"Why do you?"

"I just want to." Holly'd never let that pass.

"No good."

"I want to be close to Grandmother."

Holly curled her tongue on the corner of her upper lip. "Where did you meet him? In the park?"

Mollie gasped. Did it show that clearly?

"God, you're naive. Do you think you're the first girl to meet a guy in the park?"

"I didn't say I met a guy in the park. That's your theory."

"Come off it. What are you afraid of? Just because you haven't known him since first grade? Because you weren't formally introduced by Bonnie Bellringer's parents?" Holly looked disgusted.

"You always put me down, make me feel like a jerk."

"Grow up. Half the time you act like the kid with freckles marching across her nose in those junk books we used to read. The one who always got a date for the Senior Prom in the last chapter and lost her acne on the last page. Mollie Make-Believe days are over. They ended when Robert grew too big for the playhouse."

"You remember that?" Mollie assumed Holly had forgotten their early closeness. She had become so supercilious and scornful of the family.

"Of course. I was there too. And Robert was just as weird at the age of ten as he is now."

"Holly!"

"You sound more like your mother every day."

"Lay off my mother."

"Anyway, why do you want to stay? To go to the Senior Prom with the boy next door?" Holly raised her eyebrows and stared at her cousin.

Mollie paused. And then said carefully, selecting each word, "I met this very nice boy, you were right, in the park, and he wants me to go out with him tomorrow, and with Grandmother like this, and nobody knows him anyway, well you see that I need your help." She didn't want to describe Jaimie. Before she could say "weaving" or "left Harvard" Holly would call him "hippie." And it wouldn't help to remind her of Starshine, the guy who had come to dinner at Holly's house and then refused to eat Aunt Pat's food because he was a vegetarian. Uncle Mike still groaned about "that crazy character Holly brought home, who lives on roots and berries, like a goddamn squirrel."

"Just ask your parents if you can stay; my parents are going out tomorrow night anyway."

"Would you ask them? Sound like you want me to stay. Tell them we haven't seen each other in a long time."

"Telling me my part, writing my script, Moll?" Holly interrupted.

"Please, Holly," Mollie begged. She needed Holly's help, not her sarcasm.

"OK. Just let me handle it my own way. And don't look so dubious. I've arranged more complex things than this."

Like a secret peace treaty? Mollie thought, angered by her cousin's condescending tone. But she smiled and said, "Thanks, Holly. Have you seen Grandmother today?"

"Nobody has. Today is not a good day." Mollie fled into the bathroom with Holly's words whirling in her head. She locked the door and sat on the cold tile floor with her back against the door. "Today is not a good day." What was wrong with her? How could she have been so happy lying on the rocks with Jaimie? She should have been here, with the family. She was angry at herself because she wanted to see the loft so much, wanted to listen to Jaimie talk, wanted him to kiss her! She dug her nails into her arm. She was despicable. While Reed and Father were talking to the doctor, she was locked in the bathroom thinking about kissing a boy Grandmother didn't even know.

She unlocked the door and went to find her pocketbook. She'd wash her face, comb her hair, throw his number away, and then maybe she could face Reed and feel like a member of the family again.

Mother met her in the hall. "Mollie, you can stay at Holly's if you wish. She's feeling lonely since the twins have left."

"I don't want to, Mom. I want to stay home and work

around the house. I promised Dad I'd clean the garage."

"That's silly. Stay in town and have a good time with Holly."

"I'm sorry about the shoes."

"We're all on edge, dear." Her mother kissed her lightly. "Don't look so tragic. As you said yesterday, you can wear those shoes one more day."

Reed and her uncles were moving into the hall, preceded by the doctor, a short craggy-faced man with huge square cuff links.

"Thank you for stopping by. We'll expect you tomorrow morning." Uncle Rob stood between Reed and the doctor and lowered his voice. "Is there any significant change? Should we be prepared for any . . . developments?" Uncle Rob asked, standing in front of his father as though to shield him from the answers.

Mollie stared at the little end table next to the couch. Fresh flowers, new candy in the bowls. Who was replacing them each day? Probably Aunt Pat. What would Grandmother do when she came into the living room and saw her candy dishes filled with unrequested thin mints? Another possibility formed in Mollie's mind but she shook it away. Grandmother would be in the living room soon—probably in a couple of days.

"So you'll be a New Yorker this weekend?" Reed smiled at her and sat down. He was making an effort to be pleasant, but his face revealed the strain, his hands moved restlessly across one another in his lap. Did Reed ever cry? He had always been so firm, the head of the whole family. She wished she could make him feel better.

"Could I talk to you? Alone, Reed?"

"Let's go into the library." She loved her special talks with him. Even when she was a little girl, she had had private meetings with him. Holly never had. Neither had Nate or Robert. Just Mollie.

She settled herself into the maroon armchair and waited until Reed looked at her and was listening completely, the way he always did. "It's about Mayhew. He's very upset that he can't see Grandmother."

"He is too young, Mollie."

"He doesn't think so. And with the whole family here every day, he feels left out."

Reed frowned. "This is not a party, dear child. Grandmother is—very—ill." How ill? she thought. Why don't you tell me?

"But Mayhew wants to be here. He's not a kid anymore. You can talk to him," she added seriously.

"Your parents feel he should stay home. I agree with them."

"Mayhew feels he should be here." Something clicked. She paused, deep in thought. "It's a case of two opposing 'shoulds.'" She smiled widely, knowing that she was right. "The 'should' for Mayhew, the one that is so important to him, is that he *should* be here with Grandmother."

Reed shook his head and rubbed his eyes. "I don't quite follow you. My mind is . . . elsewhere. But I'll have a talk with your parents. Perhaps Mayhew can come in on Sunday." He kissed the top of her head as he slowly arose from his chair. "Since you seem so sure of what you're saying, I suppose I *should* go along with you."

He walked out of the room, bent forward as though he had a pain in his stomach. Mollie repeated to herself, "Two different 'shoulds.' " That was the answer. But there was only one "should" about the weekend. She should stay with Grandmother. She should not see Jaimie. She'd see him just one more time, so she would not have to wonder for the rest of her life what the loft was like. Just one more time, then she'd never see him again. She'd be with Grandmother every day after tomorrow. Robert and Nate and her aunts and uncles would be there. Reed would not be alone. And she'd visit for an hour in the morning before going to the loft. It would all work out.

She reached for the telephone to tell Hew she had arranged for him to see Grandmother, sure that Reed would have the final word with her parents. Without thinking she dialed Hilary's number instead. Hang up, she thought. No, let it ring three times. If she picks it up, talk to her; otherwise hang up.

"Hello?" Hilary. Out of breath. Running through the children's wing. It was good to hear her voice.

"Hello," Mollie said softly. What had made her dial Hilary?

"Hello, hello, who is this?"

"Hilary, it's me," Mollie said, hoping Hilary wouldn't hang up.

"Mollie?"

"Yes." Silence. "How are you?" Strained.

"Fine."

"I'm in New York at Reed's."

"How's your grandmother?"

"Not so good. None of us could see her today."

"That's too bad, Moll. I'm sorry." Silence.

"I didn't call for any special reason." Silence.

"Well, *you* called *me*."

"Could we get together some day next week? I'm staying at Holly's over the weekend."

"What for?"

"I want to talk to you, about that night."

"I'm not sure I want to talk to you." Hilary was still mad. So much had happened since that morning, Mollie could barely remember all they had said.

"I met this guy, Hil. In the park. He's going to teach me to weave. And I miss you." Talking to Hilary now was more difficult than Mollie had anticipated.

"Yeah, I miss you, except that you were dreadful." Silence. "You really hurt me, Mollie."

"I'm sorry. Please, Hil. I think I understand now. A lot has happened this week. OK?"

"OK. Have a good weekend. Hope your grandmother is better. I want to hear all about your new boy."

Mollie laughed. "Some, not all, Hil."

"What the hell has happened this week?" Hilary asked.

"Not . . . that." Mollie laughed again. "Do you love Eddie's fatigue cap? Does it make you happy just to see it?"

"God, no. It smells like rotting hair. Why?"

"No reason. I'll talk to you next week. His name is Jaimie. Have a good weekend, Hil."

Mollie hung up the phone and drew her knees up to her chest. As long as she was going to see Jaimie one last time, she might as well think about him this one last day. In private. Not in front of the family.

The door opened and Nate walked in. "What are you doing, trying to disappear into that chair?"

"Not really."

Nate sat down. "I just talked to my father. The doctor says Grandmother is getting worse. It looks bad."

"Is she . . . she is going to get better, isn't she?"

"No."

Mollie took Nate's hand. "Why don't they call another doctor to be sure?"

"They're sure, Mollie."

"Nate, I'm scared. What will Reed do?"

"I don't know."

Mollie's head was buzzing. If only Nate hadn't told her. Now she could never go down to the loft.

"Don't look like that, Moll. We have to accept it."

"What's going to happen? I mean what will it be like without Grandmother?"

"How the hell should I know? Nothing will be the same, especially Christmas." Mollie had never heard such vehemence from Nate.

"Do you think they might let me live with Reed?"

"Don't be silly, Mollie. Reed can take care of himself. And Dad and Uncle Mike are here. And your father is nearby."

"He's going to be alone."

"There's nothing any of us can do about that." He was right. No one could take Grandmother's place. But Mollie didn't want to go to Springfield anymore. She wanted to stay with Reed in Grandmother's apartment. But tomorrow she was definitely going to the loft. She lowered her head so Nate couldn't see her face.

"Hey, don't fall apart. We've got to be strong; you know, the hardy Fieldses."

"I'll try," Mollie murmured. After tomorrow, she vowed, I'll be as dependable as Nate.

"Does Holly know?"

"I'm going to tell her; we're going out for a walk."

"Why you?"

"Because I want to."

"Maybe Aunt Pat and Uncle Mike don't want her to know."

"We're not kids anymore. We have to make our own decisions."

Suddenly he grabbed her around the waist and pulled her out of the chair. "And I just decided to buy you and Holly the gooiest sundaes at Hyler's."

"Not me. I don't want to be there when you tell her."

"Suit yourself." He shrugged.

Chapter Ten

As Mollie walked downtown toward her grandparents' apartment, conflicting thoughts went through her mind. When she left their apartment today, she was going to visit an unknown boy. She was going to deceive Reed. She had never purposely done anything before without Grandmother's sanction. She said aloud as a bus roared past, drowning her words, "This is the last time. From tomorrow on, I'm going to be golden."

Her hand closed over a scrap of paper. *Nineteen Greene Street*, and brief instructions on how to get there. In two hours I'll see him. She had memorized the words on the paper but she kept reaching into her pocket, nervous that it might have slipped out, fallen onto the sidewalk and blown away.

When would Grandmother—when would it be over? If Mollie lived with Reed would the library be her room? How would they arrange things? But today came first.

Jaimie. Wandering around New York in the chilled fall air, the streets darkening earlier each day. Jaimie's loft—walls covered with beautiful paintings and brightly woven cloth, Jaimie's friends talking about art, welcoming Mollie into their group. Jaimie. She would know about weaving then. She would have designed her first pattern. Jaimie. She paused at her own reflection in the store window, lips spreading and cheeks puffing into a radiant smile.

Her scarf fluttered in the morning breeze. Mollie was glad Holly had relented and helped her dress this morning, carefully selecting items from her dazzling array of clothes. Her cousin's closet reminded her of the dress-up trunk they shared as little girls. Wearing a scarlet-patterned gypsy shirt and white flared slacks, very different from her everyday clothes, Mollie felt that same daring giddiness she had as a child, when she had paraded before the grown-ups in worn remnants of fur and threadbare brocade; clumping from Reed to Grandmother for a quick kiss; tottering in a pair of silver lamé evening shoes.

She reached the building, nodded to Edward, the doorman, checked her pocket one last time, and went upstairs.

"Good morning, Reed." She hugged him lightly. "Am I the first one here?"

"You certainly are. It's only ten o'clock."

"I wanted to see Grandmother early before everybody descends." He looked so washed out; she would be doing the right thing to live with him. This was a good time to tell him, before the whole family arrived.

"The nurse is giving her a bath now. We have a new one, a real crackerjack, Mrs. Withers."

"I have some shopping to do, but I'd like to talk to you first." *Nineteen Greene Street.* She looked at her grandfather guiltily. "Tomorrow I can stay with Grandmother all day. Aunt Pat said she'd be down soon. Uncle Mike too."

"Fine, dear. Let's go into the library." No mention of her gypsy costume or the trailing chiffon scarf Holly had impulsively knotted around her neck as she was leaving. "You go on in, Mollie dear, I'm going to check on Grandmother. I'll be right with you." He moved so slowly!

Maybe Holly had been right. Jaimie should have met her uptown. But she didn't want to seem like a kid who had to be picked up and delivered. If she got lost, she could always get a cab. And riding the unfamiliar subway would make the day even more like an adventure.

Holly's reaction had been surprising. After talking to Jaimie, Mollie had gone into Holly's room and repeated the plans she had just made. She was surprised that Holly did not mention her talk with Nate, but as usual Mollie picked up the cue and avoided any mention of Grandmother.

"Where?"

"At his loft. On Greene Street."

"Where the hell is Greene Street?"

"Downtown. I have the directions."

"He's not going to pick you up?" Holly's eyebrows went up.

"Of course not. I am sixteen, you may recall."

"When was the last time you went to Greene Street?" She bent her head and started brushing her hair.

"I told you he gave me directions."

Holly straightened up and tossed her hairbrush across the room. "You're flipping out. I thought you wanted to have a date. I didn't know it was to be a rendezvous—or I would never have gotten involved."

"*You* do it." Mollie challenged her.

111

"I'm used to it."

"I have to start sometime."

"I agree. A sneaky date with a boy is one thing—but going alone to his *loft* in some unheard-of part of town is crazy."

"Just because you haven't heard of Greene Street, plenty of people have." Who was Holly to start acting like her mother? Holly's whole life had been one big secret—ever since she had copied her book reports from the jacket flaps.

"You are going to be back before dark," Holly said calmly.

"C'mon, Holly. This is my one day."

"Why, where is this loft-lothario going?"

"I mean because of Grandmother and everything. I can't go haring down there all the time."

"You could if you knew how," Holly challenged her. "I'm for jazzing up your life, but not all in one day. You don't know enough."

"And I suppose you know everything?"

"Almost. And I think faster."

"Well, I'm taking a crash course."

"You have enough money for a cab if things get hairy?"

"Things aren't going to get hairy. You don't know Jaimie. He's not like that."

"Like what?"

"What you're thinking."

Holly groaned. "I'm not concerned about things being hairy for Jaimie. I'm sure he can handle himself. But you still turn into a pumpkin at midnight."

"I do not," Mollie said softly, thinking of the violent reactions she'd had about Hilary and Eddie. But that was because Hilary had lied to her, and never told her about Eddie. "Look, Holly, just don't say anything. I've told Aunt Pat I'm going shopping." Holly had to agree. Mollie could still hear Jaimie's voice, "See you at noon, Little Red."

"While you're shopping, you'd better hope they have a sale on smarts. You need to stock up."

"*I* never had to have a special tutor."

"Right, Mollie. Why don't you show what's-his-name how to do the binomial theorem?" Holly thought she knew everything. But she was not going to ruin tomorrow.

Reed sat down across from her, interrupting her thoughts. "Tell me, Mollie Make-Believe, what's on your mind?" He leaned toward her, resting his arms on his knees as he had so many times when they had had their special private conferences. Often Mollie had asked to see him alone, not because she had something secret to tell him but because she loved to talk to him alone, not sharing him with the rest of the family.

"I want to come and live here with you. I mean—after —when—" She faltered, waiting for him to finish her sentence.

"But, Mollie, you're set to go to Springfield."

"I don't want to go to Springfield. I want us to live together here."

"You'll like the college once you get there. It's generous of you to want to live with me, and I appreciate your thought, but you must live your own life."

"I would be miserable there, thinking of you all alone here." It had never occurred to her that Reed might object.

"We'll discuss it with your parents." He passed his hand slowly across his face. Mollie's nervousness grew as they sat in silence. She wanted so to help him. She caught her breath and began to talk very fast.

"Holly and I had the best time last night. We talked and watched television until all hours. Aunt Pat and Uncle Mike went out to dinner, you know. Uncle Mike said the duck was stringy and the mousse tasted like common pudding. He almost killed the newspaper at breakfast. I love staying with them. Spending the night there is still the same as when we were little." He seemed to be listening, so Mollie continued at top speed. "The twins left their blankets. Aunt Pat will have to mail them special delivery this morning; Uncle Mike said they should freeze for a while; teach them responsibility. Then he called the weather to find out how cold it was going to be in Vermont, and started to lay out these elaborate plans for getting them blankets."

Reed nodded his head. "That's the way he is." They sat quietly and then Reed winked at her. "Mayhew is coming in tomorrow with your parents."

She reached out and hugged her grandfather. "Thanks, Reed. I can always count on you."

"We'll talk more about this idea of yours, Mollie dear. But you must learn to live your own life."

"I know that. And I will be living my own life. I'll just be living it here instead of at Springfield. Honestly, Reed, it's what I want to do."

A muffled cough from the other side of the wall made Reed leap from his chair. "I must go in to Grandmother," he said abruptly as he ran from the room.

Mollie sighed. She had made the right decision. Now she

could visit Jaimie. The sun would be filling the loft, shining on all his paintings. Would there be floor-to-ceiling bookshelves? *Nineteen Greene Street.* A cheerful "Good morning" to Grandmother, and then she would be free for the whole day.

Mollie paused at the door of Grandmother's room. Shocked, she stared at the scene in front of her. How could Grandmother have changed so in these few days? She looked so frail; her cheeks had become deep holes, and her beautiful hair was lifeless on the pillow. Reed was bent close to her, holding her hand and talking in the low intimate voice she had heard for more than fifty years. Was he seeing her as a young girl, or a busy mother before her three sons had left home? Would he remember this caved-in face as Grandmother? Mollie squeezed her eyes shut and clutched her stomach until the pain helped steady her. She opened her eyes and forced herself to watch. If only there would be a miraculous improvement, if only Grandmother herself would emerge gustily from the heap in the bed. Overwhelmed, Mollie left the room and hurried from the building. She didn't slow down until she was surrounded by the giant skyscrapers of a different New York, where the image of Grandmother dissolved into crowds of Saturday shoppers and city-struck tourists. Gradually the medicinal smell left her nostrils and Mollie gave herself to the brilliance of an untroubled summer day.

Walk to subway . . . change at Fourteenth Street . . . walk to corner—the directions seemed endless and it was now almost eleven thirty. Mollie stepped into the street, hailed a taxi, and silently thanked Holly for slipping her ten dollars at breakfast.

"Nineteen Greene Street." She hoped she sounded authoritative. If the driver thought she was a rube, he might take her by way of Brooklyn. She leaned forward slightly to make sure the slippery silk vest would not get wrinkled against the back of the seat.

"Should I take the Drive?"

"I usually do." She hoped she was right.

As the taxi sped down the Drive, which followed the curving East River, Mollie reran the picture of Jaimie's loft, revising her conception to include brightly patterned Navaho rugs and a white paper lantern swaying in the morning breeze.

The cabbie turned off the Drive and Mollie looked out the window at darkened warehouses and deserted streets. No people. No pokey thin trees opposite canopied doorways, just cracked sidewalks and shabby square buildings with mammoth, many-paned dusty windows. Would Jaimie's friends like her? Would they come to visit at Reed's apartment?

"You want to get out here, lady? Walk over a block? Otherwise I gotta go all the way around cause this is one way." Mollie fumbled for her wallet; she'd much rather walk the final block. If Jaimie were looking out the window, she didn't want him to see her arrive in a taxi, like some feeble old lady. "Right straight down this block?" she asked the driver.

"Go to the next corner. Turn left; halfway down that slanting street. They don't have regular blocks down here. You sure you know where you're going?"

"Certainly. I just have to get my bearings." She retied her scarf, smiled at the driver in the rearview mirror, and got out of the cab, eager to find Jaimie, eager for him to see there was a gypsy side to her.

She walked to the end of the block. But she couldn't locate number nineteen. She crossed the street. The other side of the block had a huge driveway with a red-and-white moving truck backed into its two-story garage. She hoped Jaimie wasn't watching from his window; she felt foolish searching the deserted street. The whole block looked like one over-grown building with several doorways. When he had said the loft resembled an airplane hangar, she had thought it was a joke. She crossed the street again and looked for a number all along the molding of the warped wooden door. She tried to open it, pushed against it with her shoulder, in the hope of checking the names on the mailboxes in the hall-way. But the door wouldn't budge, and the doorknob merely wiggled in its socket. Damn, how will I ever find him? It looks as though nobody's lived here in years, she thought angrily. As she walked to the next entrance, wishing she had met Jaimie in the park, she heard her name. She looked over her shoulder and there was Jaimie ambling toward her, as though he were used to seeing her there.

She raised her hand, smiled, and tossed her scarf over her shoulder like a wild gypsy princess.

"Hi. You look great."

"My Saturday clothes." Mollie touched her vest casually. He was wearing his Staten Island T-shirt. It made her feel as though she had known him a long time.

"I was just heading to the store to get some milk."

"Where is there a store? It doesn't look as though anyone's been here since the Dutch left in 1664."

"You'd be surprised. Inside all these lofts are hundreds of

117

people—some quite lofty," he added with a smile.

She took his hand. "I'm excited. I can't wait to learn to weave."

"It'll take more than one day, you know. Just threading the loom will take longer than that."

"Oh." She tried to hide her disappointment.

"Did you expect to go home with a bolt of cloth under your arm, Litle Red?" He grinned.

"Of course not." But she had hoped to bring home to Holly a small piece of intricately patterned cloth, proof of her new life, her private explorations down to Greene Street.

"Here, my little friend, is a milk store." He guided her into a tiny store with a worn linoleum floor, showing splintery wood planks around the doorway where the dim green marble pattern had completely disappeared. The dark room, lit only by two bare lightbulbs swinging from exposed rafters in the plaster ceiling, was crowded with squeaking metal racks of magazines and comics, their covers obliterated by flopping curled-over pages. Piles of newspapers lined the counters; cheap windup toys were scattered on top of the papers, in borders along the floor. Sagging wooden shelves crammed with dusty cans and long boxes of pasta reached all the way to the ceiling. A ladder was propped against one of the shelves.

"Everything but milk," she whispered in the cool damp half-darkness. She ignored the stares of two swarthy men in short-sleeved white shirts standing behind the counter.

"Keep walking," Jaimie said, his hand on her waist, "and you'll hit the milk."

"If it doesn't hit me first. Is this stuff safe?" She frowned, looking down into a freezer holding a jumble of milk cartons, ice-cream containers, and a few single sticks of butter.

He laughed and paid for the milk and some ice cream. "Let's hurry before it melts."

"The milk?"

"It's the same milk you drink uptown. We've only had three deaths from it this month." They walked back into the bright light. It's probably filth that makes that store so dark, she thought. But she smiled at Jaimie.

He took her hand and led her back down the windy littered street. As he unlocked the door to number nineteen, which did not have a number outside, she straightened her scarf in case Jaimie's friends were waiting inside.

He opened the door and stood aside for her to enter. She stood in the doorway, not quite focusing for a moment. It did look like an airplane hangar, only there was no airplane taking up lots of room. The windows were two stories high, and the hard summer light was shining in—on what? A few stalky plants clustered under the window; a rocking chair with a pillow thrown across its buckling seat; a long low table covered with Magic Markers, colored paper, fat twisted Day-Glo-colored yarn; a bed almost square in shape raised off the floor by cement blocks; and acres of bare wooden floor.

She turned, hopefully, in the other direction. A two-burner stove, rusty-white sink, and waist-high refrigerator lined the short wall opposite the windows; near them, a fish-patterned plastic shower curtain hung in a three-foot circle from the ceiling. A couple of half-painted canvases were tacked to the wall, the white of the canvas standing out from the yellow oldness of the wall on which they hung. Streaks of paint ran

119

off the canvas onto the wall as though to blend the two together.

"Where's the loom?" she asked.

"Across the hall at Elida's. We'll get it later."

Elida? She had never thought Jaimie might have a girl friend! "Is she a weaver too?"

"She weaves," he answered.

Where should she sit? Floor? Rocking chair? She had never been in a boy's apartment. She had seen David's room at school, and she and Holly had visited Nate at Harvard. But that was very different from this cavernous space, silent except for Jaimie setting the coffeepot on the stove. She walked toward the bed, pretending to study the canvas tacked above it. Should she sit on the bed? It seemed much larger now that she was close to it, but everything was dwarfed in this place.

"Take a pillow and sit at the table." Jaimie put two thick pottery mugs of coffee on the table and dropped easily to the floor. "Want to make some collages?" She didn't answer. She felt as though she were in kindergarten, seated at this table piled high with cutout triangles and circles and paste and pencils and pens.

Jaimie held up an animal made from three triangles of black paper, with weird wool orange horns and a red circle mouth. "What do you think of my beast?"

"Fantastic," Mollie answered. Under the table she was digging her fingers into her palms. She had lied to Reed, left Grandmother, to look at colored-paper monsters that she could have seen on the twins' bulletin board that morning.

"Where are your paintings and drawings, Jaimie?"

"Two of my canvases are up there." He pointed to the

walls. "My sketch books are around somewhere, but let's not play Show-and-Tell. Here's a pair of scissors; the glue is on the table someplace."

Mollie snatched a piece of paper from the table and started cutting squares.

"Why green? Remind you of the park?

"I don't know. I hadn't thought about it." She hadn't even noticed it was green; it was the closest piece to her. "I don't much feel like doing cutouts." She stood up and walked down to the window. Holly would die laughing—big trip to the mysterious loft. Could she handle herself? In this branch of a Head Start playroom? What had happened to the Jaimie from the park? She looked over her shoulder, saw him bent over a piece of blue paper.

She walked back toward the center of the room and sat down on the bed.

"Are you depressed, Mollie?" Jaimie handed her a primitive bluebird. "Will this help?" I wish it would, she thought. "Is it your grandmother?"

"Yeah, I guess so. I've decided to live with my grandfather and go to school here. I told him this morning." Maybe if they started talking, she would regain the closeness they had had in the park.

"You're throwing away a great time in Boston."

"New York isn't the sticks." She looked at his arms. The small blond hairs didn't show, but she knew they were there, knew without having to see them. She lay back, staring at the ceiling, her anger flowing out of her. She hummed softly, idly. Jaimie seemed distant here, he hadn't touched her or looked at her the way he had at the bear cave. She heard Jaimie stand up, knew he was walking toward her, but she

121

kept her eyes fixed on the ceiling as though she were not aware of him. He sat close to her, his hip almost touching hers. She was momentarily startled by the nearness of his face. His eyes were huge; his head massive. As he smiled at her slowly, a smile that was mostly in his eyes, she felt a ripple in her stomach. She was back in the park.

She reached up and touched his hair. Soft. "Will you be in New York this year?"

"I don't know yet." He traced a line down the length of her nose. She shivered. Jaimie bent to kiss her and she closed her eyes. He smelled faintly of cloves; she hadn't noticed that in the park. Her mind drifted and she kissed Jaimie and he kissed her. And she thought, it must be awfully hot in here; I'm beginning to sweat. Jaimie's lips were soft and she relaxed against his chest, comfortable, floating. Perfect. Her hand pressing Jaimie's back was damp. He was sweating too. Lightly.

Jaimie shifted and stretched out, one leg sliding between hers. Pictures were forming quickly in her mind. Jaimie undressed. Herself undressed. Lying naked on the bed in this isolated cavernous room. She twisted her head to one side, but she couldn't move from beneath him. She caught her breath. I'm trapped, she thought.

Jaimie turned her head back toward him and kissed her again. His hand was outlining her body as it moved downward. An awareness of Jaimie's hand opening her slacks! God, make him stop. As if in answer to her prayer, Jaimie rolled over and stretched his hands far over his head. Mollie sighed in relief. He sat up, took off his T-shirt and tossed it on the floor. Mollie felt dizzy. He seemed like a total stranger. She turned away from his bare chest and stood up.

"I have to go to the john," she whispered, buttoning her slacks.

"Behind the curtain, Little Red."

Even his voice sounded different. She hoped for time to think, but behind the plastic curtain she felt as though she were still on the bed with Jaimie. She looked closely at her hands, turning them over and over. There wasn't even a mirror in here to comb her hair, see her face. If only she could see her own reflection, reassure herself that nothing had changed. She examined her thumb, touched the fingernail broken this morning, still jagged. I'm all right, she told herself. I broke that nail at breakfast with Holly. The thought seemed to calm her.

She returned to the room, relieved that her hands had stopped trembling. She did not want Jaimie to know how frightened she had been. He hadn't moved; he was sprawled on the bed, leaning on one elbow. She hesitated. He reached out quickly and pulled her down onto the bed. Slivers of scenes from books and movies flashed into her mind, but none fitted exactly. Her mind closed, empty as a drive-in in winter.

As Jaimie leaned across her, she spoke quickly, before he could kiss her. "Where's the loom, Jaimie? Why don't we get started?"

"We are started," he murmured. His hair was almost covering her face. She tried to brush it away. They were kissing again. She had to stop it. His hand returned to her slacks, fiddling with the buttons. What could she do? She couldn't let him find out she didn't know anything.

She put her hand on his shoulder and gave a slight push. Nothing. She pushed him again, harder. "That's enough,

Jaimie," she whispered, surprised at the tininess of her voice. She was jangling inside, edgy as though a firecracker had unexpectedly exploded behind her.

"Don't be afraid," he said, smoothing her hair. "Remember the cave." He held her tight against him. Neither of them moved. She buried her face deep into his shoulder to stop the sensation of falling, the terror she had felt at the bear cave. She was soothed by the steady rhythm of his breathing, but she could not dispel the fear.

"Mollie, believe." He looked at her intensely.

"I can't, Jaimie; I can't." Her voice quavered.

He rolled to the other side of the bed and stared at the ceiling. "Mollie Make-Believe," he said, a hard edge to his gentle voice.

The spectacular vest was rumpled; her scarf was wrinkled. She had to get home.

"Jaimie, I've got to go. . . ."

"Not to your grandmother's!" he exclaimed in mock surprise.

"Well, she is sick." Mollie said. Maybe there'd still be time to visit Grandmother. She tried to cover her hands with her scarf; she didn't want Jaimie to see them shaking.

Mollie got up. She went to the window, looked out at the empty street. Why doesn't he say something? Will he ever want to see me again? Will we ever go to the park together? If she didn't leave immediately, she'd be crying.

"Good-bye, Jaimie."

He didn't move from the bed. "Good-bye, Mollie." She paused at the door.

"Maybe I'll see you in the park," she offered tentatively.

"Maybe. When you can manage the bear cave."

She left the loft, his words sounding over and over in her head. She ran down the block, calling "Grandmother, Grandmother." She found a taxi and settled herself inside, gripping her hands.

She rolled down the window and let the air blow on her burning face. She closed her eyes, drained and tired as though she had been running for a long time.

Chapter Eleven

Mollie was lying on Holly's bed, showered, sipping lemonade. She had been a fool to go to the loft; she would never see Jaimie again. It serves me right for lying and sneaking around, she thought. Holly burst through the door.

"Oh, there you are. Clara said you got home an hour ago. Are you OK?" Holly bounced down on the bed.

"I'm fine. I just went to see a boy, not have open-heart surgery," she snapped.

"How was it, the loft of your dreams?"

"We had a nice time."

"That must be why you look like you're about to cry."

"I'm fine, fine." Her voice rose to a shout.

"I won't say another word. Why don't you go out with Treacle and me tonight?"

"No."

"Well, I might as well stay home too. I need a rest from Britain's greatest export."

"Go out with him, Holly."

Holly raised her eyebrows and stared at her cousin, wrapped in an afghan on a summer day, hugging the far side of the bed. "We'll watch television and make the Nazi fix us something extreme for dinner since Mom and Dad will be out. What shall we have?"

Mollie shrugged.

"OK, I'll tell her to surprise us, as long as it's steak and chocolate." Holly looked at Mollie's eyes, half-closed and glistening with tears. "Why don't you take a nap?"

"Stop babying me," she said automatically. She pulled the afghan tighter around her and smiled at Holly. "Well, maybe one of Grandmother's catnaps."

"It's all grist for the mill, Mollie." She lowered the shades and gave her cousin an affectionate pat. "Don't be too worried about this afternoon. I told you last night, you can't do everything in one day."

"Are you coming down to Reed's this morning?" Mollie had said little all last evening. She had felt awkward with Holly, who as usual seemed to know all the answers. Now, seated at breakfast, Mollie wanted to bridge the gap across yesterday, cover over the helplessness she had shown to Holly.

"Later." Holly was reading the Sunday paper and absently stirring her coffee. Mollie was struck by Holly's strong resemblence to Aunt Pat. Holly was so completely her own person, it was difficult to think of her as Aunt Pat and Uncle Mike's daughter. Her aunt came into the dining room, still calling to her husband.

"I don't think Reed has had a hot meal in a week. We

have to maintain some degree of order. Cyn and John want to eat early so they can drive home at a decent hour." His answer was muffled.

"Good morning, girls. We're all going to have dinner at Reed's at five."

"Who's all?" Holly asked, not looking up.

"The family, dear."

"What fun." Mollie handed her the basket of croissants and smiled gaily. Aunt Pat sliced herself a square of butter, while her niece watched her admiringly. Her hair was perfectly combed and her face looked as though she had been up for hours. In the morning Mother looked as if her blood had been drained away during the night. Mollie looked down at her hands; they looked gray and stubby next to her aunt's pink-polished long ring-laden fingers. Jewelry was as essential a part of her aunt as an ornate gilt frame is to a Renaissance madonna.

"Mrs. Withers is with Grandmother, and it will give us a chance to sit down together, the whole family, instead of you children running to a coffee shop and Reed pacing around the apartment holding a sandwich, and the rest of us hunting through the refrigerator for a snack to tide us over until we leave."

"When will my parents be in?" Mollie asked, wanting to keep the conversation going.

"Around noon, dear. But there's no need for you and Holly to go down until midafternoon. You can both help me carry the food. It will be much simpler to have Clara prepare it here and take it down there hot."

"I think I'll go down earlier if it's OK," Mollie said, interrupting. She was anxious to talk to Reed. "But I'll come back and help you carry stuff. Unless you want me to help cook." Holly gave her a filthy glance. Mollie sighed. Holly had been so nice last night.

Aunt Pat left the room to call Aunt Cathy, a list already taking shape in her mind. It would be like old times. Mollie grinned. "Hey, Holly, think they'll make us eat first?"

"No, Mollie, we eat with the grown-ups now." Holly threw her napkin across her plate and left the room.

Mollie didn't want to start a duel with Holly so she called good-bye to her aunt and uncle through their closed bedroom door and left the apartment. And Jaimie's last words to her went through her head. Maybe one day she would manage the bear cave, but she couldn't imagine climbing to the peak, that configuration of sun-bleached rocks that rose so forbiddingly in her mind.

Mollie felt lonely, walking down the street, no one near her. When they had been little girls, Holly had walked with Grandmother, and Mollie with Reed. She had tucked her arm through her grandfather's, trying to imitate her grandmother's stately steps. She was a queen going to her coronation, walking proudly beside Reed. If only Reed were here now, talking quietly, commenting on the paintings in the gallery windows, naming the precious jewels shining from their black-velvet backdrops as they passed by. It wouldn't be long now. She and Reed would walk together when she lived with him, and this lonely, empty feeling would disappear.

When she arrived at the apartment, a new doorman stopped her. "Yes, Miss?" he asked, blocking her way.

"I'm going to see my grandfather," she said coldly. Where was Edward?

"Who is your grandfather?"

"Mr. Fields," Mollie snapped, close to tears. "I am Mollie Fields." Everyone here knew who she was.

"I'll anounce you."

Reed will kill him, Mollie thought angrily. Upstairs, Mrs. Withers, the nurse, opened the door. "Where is my grandfather?" Mollie asked.

"He's with Doctor."

Mollie's shoulders drooped. "May I see my grandmother?" she asked in a small voice.

"She's not awake, dear."

"Is she better today?"

"Excuse me. I must join Doctor."

Just as Mollie sat on the couch, the doorbell rang. She got up to answer it. Soon she would be answering this door all the time.

"Nate, Robert." She smiled at them.

"Mollie Make-Believe, is it you?" Nate twirled her into the living room.

"Shhhh. You'll wake Grandmother."

"I doubt it," Robert said.

"The nurse said she's asleep." Mollie was glad to have more specific information than Robert.

"As good a word as any, although highly inaccurate. As most euphemisms are." Robert walked into the kitchen without looking at Nate or Mollie.

"What the hell is he talking about?"

Nate led her to the window. "Grandmother is in a coma. It's close now, Moll."

"That's not true. She's asleep. Ask the nurse. Robert is not an authority."

"Believe what you want, but prepare yourself, Moll." Nate went to join his brother.

The library door opened and the doctor walked out, Reed on one side of him and Uncle Rob on the other. They paused for a moment in the living room, talking softly, Reed nodding his head in a regular rocking motion. She was relieved that no one noticed her; the sight of the doctor unnerved her. She tiptoed into the kitchen.

"What's going to happen, Nate?" She reached out her arms.

"You know as much as we do, Mollie." Nate hugged her. But Robert started doodling on Grandmother's grocery pad.

"Grandmother won't like you using up her pad," Mollie said. Both boys stared at her. She shivered and buried her face in Nate's shoulder. "Damn, damn, damn." Her words were muffled.

"Don't fall apart, Mollie."

All day she felt herself withdrawing from the actions of the family. Her parents arrived; her mother left to join Aunt Pat. Mayhew, his face ashen, stood on the edge of the circle of Reed, the uncles, and Father. It must be horrible for him, Mollie thought, trying to stir herself to comfort her brother. Because he hasn't been coming here every day, he's not used to the hushed atmosphere. She sank back into her chair. Had Mayhew been allowed to see Grandmother? She doubted it since Grandmother still seemed to be sleeping, her door closed. Only Reed had gone into the room today, as far as Mollie knew.

Holly was looking out the window, her body pressed

against the sill, as though she were trying to escape from the room. Mollie didn't even attempt to talk to her. Finally she forced herself to wind wool for Aunt Cathy.

The afternoon passed in muted silence, each person isolated in a corner of the room. They were all startled by the clatter at the door as Aunt Pat and Mother entered the apartment, laden with plastic containers and covered bowls. The doorman followed them, balancing a glazed ham on a silver platter. Mollie's throat closed at the sight of the food. I couldn't possibly eat and be pleasant. I can't watch Reed eat, she thought.

"Mollie, please help Holly set the table. And arrange the vegetables on this large plate."

"Grandmother uses that plate for cakes," Mollie answered her mother.

"Mollie, do as I tell you."

"How can you all eat? I don't want any dinner."

"We must keep things on an even keel," her mother said. "This—this condition could last for days, even weeks. Now please do as I told you. We don't need any prima donnas here." Mother's whisper had turned into a hiss.

"I'll sit in the living room. Just leave me alone."

"John, come and talk to Mollie for me," Mother called.

"I don't feel like eating, Dad. I just want to sit in the living room alone." Father's face told her that he wasn't particularly interested in her eating dinner. His eyes had the same squint Mayhew's got when her brother was about to cry.

She walked back to the living room, deserted except for Reed and Uncle Mike. She watched Uncle Mike coax Reed toward the dining room. They walked a few steps, Uncle Mike's hand lightly pushing the back of his father's arm.

They stopped; Reed shook his head, Uncle Mike dropped his hand. They talked and the sequence repeated itself until gradually Reed crossed the threshhold into the dining room.

Mollie looked at the ornaments on the tables, some of them pushed aside by unfamiliar candy bowls and flower vases. When she had been little, she used to hold a piece of her skirt in each hand so that she would not be tempted to touch any of the precious objects. She almost heard Grandmother's voice saying sharply, "Don't touch that," as her hand closed over a smooth jade elephant. She picked him up, enjoying the coolness of the stone. Very lightly she touched the tip of his trunk. Immediately she replaced him on his mahogany stand under the lamp, as though to avoid further temptation. Guiltily she looked up and was surprised to find herself alone, unobserved. From the stunning silence in the room she realized that she would soon be able to hold the little elephant whenever she wished. She missed Grandmother's watchfulness already. Whenever she had been allowed to lift the cover of the ginger jar to smell the rose potpourri, Mollie had felt that she could not possibly drop the porcelain top as long as Grandmother stood nearby, almost guiding her hand. Mollie rubbed her hand absently trying to recapture Grandmother's vital essence, a power strong enough to destroy all Mollie's fears.

"I'm going to have my dinner now." Mollie jumped at the low voice. Mrs. Withers nodded at her pleasantly.

"How's my grandmother?" asked Mollie, feeling as though she were in charge while Reed was eating dinner.

"No change," Mrs. Withers answered automatically and turned to go into the kitchen.

She had to talk to Grandmother while everybody was at dinner. No one would know that she was sitting on Grandmother's bed. She stared at the mound next to her. Grandmother's hair was a mass of fuzzy wisps; her lips almost gone. But Mollie was not frightened. She picked up her grandmother's hand. It was soft, almost padded, the fingers curling gently. No nail polish, but Grandmother's hand.

"Grandmother, I have to talk to you." The still body remained motionless; the shallow breaths barely moved the sheet. But Mollie felt secure. She continued calmly.

"I met this boy, his name is Jaimie. He went to Harvard; Nate doesn't know him. He is an artist and he knows how to weave." She paused, gripped Grandmother's hand more tightly, and continued softly, "I really like him. He lives in a loft." She paused. "It's not a good idea, is it, Grandmother?" Stroking Grandmother's hand, Mollie was walking in the park, stroking Grandmother's fur coat, watching the rainbows her rings cast in the winter sun. "Grandmother, I'll never see him again. I promise I won't go to the park alone except—no, I won't go to the park again." She was crying now, silent tears that didn't stop her voice. "I won't see him. I'm sorry, I'm sorry, I'm sorry."

Someone was touching Mollie's shoulder, pulling her away from Grandmother. "Leave me alone," she shouted, her tears becoming violent. "I have to talk to Grandmother. Leave me alone. I'm staying here." Mollie struggled helplessly against the determined clamplike hands of Mrs. Withers, and then ran to Reed, who was standing in the doorway.

"Tell them,' she sobbed, "tell them, I'm staying here. Tell them I don't have to leave."

Chapter Twelve

Aunt Pat handed Mollie an unfolded lace handkerchief as soon as they had settled into the back of the cab. Mollie let it drift feather-light into her lap. She waited for her mother and her aunt to ask about her going in to Grandmother. She couldn't explain it; she didn't know why it had become so important to talk to Grandmother, to be near her. And Mollie was too tired to think about it. But neither Mother nor Aunt Pat said a thing, at first.

As they drove uptown everything looked two-dimensional, touched with a coating of technicolor. Mollie stared out the window, hoping the ache inside her would stop. Then Mollie caught a few of Mother's words. "You must be overtired. You need some rest. I can't imagine why you would do such a thing." Aunt Pat remained silent.

They pulled to a stop in front of Aunt Pat's building. Aunt Pat picked up her unused handkerchief, paid the driver, and stepped from the cab with her usual unhesitating efficiency. Mother stood on the sidewalk, looking uncomfortable, as though she were waiting to sneeze. Mollie pulled herself across the seat to the door, trying to avoid her mother's frowning face.

"Cyn, why don't you go back and see about John and the others? You have a long drive ahead of you. I'll take care of Mollie." Mother nodded; she seemed relieved as she got back in the cab. Mollie was amazed. She looked at her mother questioningly. No explanations?

"Good night, dear. I think a good night's sleep . . ." Her voice was soaked up by the taxi squeaking away from the curb. Mollie trailed Aunt Pat across the lobby, concentrating on the rhythm of their shoes against the highly polished marble floor.

"C'mon, Mollie, the elevator's here." Aunt Pat was as calm as though Mollie hadn't just shocked the whole family, hadn't had to be forcibly pried away from Reed and bundled off so that she could no longer "add to the highly charged atmosphere," as Uncle Rob had put it.

"Why don't you take a bath and I'll fix you a tray?" Aunt Pat was walking rapidly through the living room, turning on lamps, drawing the pendulous drapes, and pausing beside a geranium to twist off a brown leaf.

"I'm not hungry." Mollie flopped down on the couch.

Aunt Pat sat across from her. "What about a glass of milk?"

"I don't know why I had to talk to Grandmother." Mollie paused. It might be easier to try to explain to Aunt Pat. She never got as upset as Mother, and besides then Aunt Pat would tell the rest of the family and Mollie would not have to face their displeasure. She dug her hands under the sofa cushion, paused for a few minutes and began.

136

"Jaimie is this boy I met in the park. I wasn't supposed to be there. I met him when I was supposed to be buying shoes." Mollie rubbed one foot on top of the other and tried to read her aunt's reaction.

"Mollie, you don't have to tell me about this boy. You're growing up and you have a right to some privacy." Mollie stared at her, not comprehending. Aunt Pat must not have understood what she had said.

"But I had to tell Grandmother. She may die, and she knows everything about me. She always knows, and—" Mollie stopped. It was odd, sitting in Aunt Pat's living room talking about Grandmother, but her aunt could explain everything to the rest of the family. Mollie couldn't face that alone.

Once before Aunt Pat had come to her rescue. In seventh grade Mollie had refused to go to gym class, and the teacher had called Mother when Aunt Pat and Uncle Mike were visiting. Mother had been furious, a line of white rage around her upper lip. But Aunt Pat had laughed and said, "Well, I'm glad to see Mollie has finally refused to do something. She gets plenty of exercise riding and fencing. Tell them she's been ill and let it go." Surprisingly they did. Remembering this, Mollie continued, "And even this weekend. I only stayed here—"

"I really don't want to hear all this, Mollie." Aunt Pat came over to the couch and sat close to her niece. "You have a right to keep things to yourself. Not because you must hide what you are doing, not because what you are doing is wrong, but because you have to begin living your own life."

"Try telling my parents that," Mollie said ruefully.

"They know it, dear. It's hard for parents to let go; parents like things to remain the same as much as children do."

Mollie looked at her closely. She was amazed at the turn the conversation was taking.

"You are becoming an adult, and gradually the family, and even your friends, will know less and less about your daily activities."

"It's already started," Mollie said quietly, thinking of Hilary and Eddie.

"Remember when you and Holly used to ask Grandmother to tell you when you would be grown up?" Mollie nodded. "Do you remember what she answered?"

"She never did answer us. She just laughed and said, 'When you stop asking.' "

"That *was* the answer. When you are living by your own rules, you don't have to ask anybody—and you are an adult."

"I don't have any rules. I have Grandmother's rules, Reed's rules, and Mother and Dad's. . . ." Mollie ticked them off on her fingers.

"We all share our rules with you so that you will know how we think life should be lived. But when you are an adult you will be making your own decisions about how you live. And there will be no reason to hide anything, because you won't be breaking anybody's rules but your own. And you can't keep secrets from yourself."

"All that freedom, living by my own rules, doing anything I want . . . with nobody knowing . . . all alone." Mollie suddenly was sobbing hysterically. She fell against her aunt like a bird crashing into a windowpane. She felt Aunt Pat's arms holding her, knew her tears were soaking into her aunt's dress.

She was alone, shapeless, formless.

Finally her stringy voice. "She's going to die. She'll never know if I study hard, she'll never hold hands under the table with Reed, she'll never sit on this couch, and," Mollie shook her head fiercely and screamed, "she'll never know who I marry."

"No, she won't. But you'll know if she would like the boy. And that is what Grandmother is leaving behind. Each of us knows what her rules are—what she would do in a given situation."

"We know her cloth. We know what patterns she would weave," Mollie said softly, suddenly soothed.

"What?" Aunt Pat leaned toward her.

"Grandmother's cloth is like an Impressionist painting, with some salmon-colored poppies." Mollie leaned back and closed her eyes. She couldn't picture her own cloth, couldn't see what patterns it would form. Jaimie's paper bluebird, Grandmother's jewels, Holly's dark hair. It will not be the same as Grandmother's or anyone else's because I will be weaving things only I know about, private things, she thought.

"Mollie?"

"I wish I could see my own cloth," she said drowsily.

"Mollie, what are you saying?"

"It's private, Aunt Pat, not secret, private."

"Now, you go and take a bath while I check the refrigerator."

"Could I have some cocoa and cinnamon toast?"

"I think it can be arranged."

Lying in the tub, a warm wet washcloth covering her face, Mollie concentrated greedily on the collages flashing through her mind. Holly's cloth woven with metallic threads, glittery and tough; Hilary's a flowery patchwork. But that just reflected the part of them Mollie knew about. She sat up suddenly, swirls of soapy water swishing on each side of her.

"Aunt Pat?" she called, some of the strength back in her voice.

"Yes, dear." She sounded crisp, everyday, again.

"Is that why Holly is allowed to date wild boys, because she's making her own rules?" Mollie shouted through the door.

Aunt Pat opened the door, handed Mollie a towel, and began straightening the bathroom as she talked. "You know, dear, you're not going to wake up one morning with your own set of rules, like the printed set in the Monopoly box. And neither is Holly. Uncle Mike and I tell Holly what we think, she knows how we feel about what she does, but she must decide for herself what she's going to do."

"My parents would never buy that. They still treat me like a child, a ten-year-old."

"You have to take it for yourself. Remember what Grandmother always told you, 'When you stop asking'?" She paused to align the bottles on a wicker shelf. "When you are ready, you will stop asking, and begin deciding. You'll begin getting some practice this fall when you go away to school. Because we won't all be around for you to ask."

"I'm going to live with Reed. Because of Grandmother . . ." Mollie stared up at her aunt, who was scrubbing out the sink and polishing the faucets with an old stiff washcloth she had discovered behind the wastebasket.

"Oh?"

"Yes. I really want to," she added.

"Fine," Aunt Pat answered blandly. "But for now, get out of that cold water and put on your nightgown. You need some sleep and I want to get back to Reed's."

"Will you wait until I drink my cocoa?"

"Sure."

Mollie settled into bed and sipped her cocoa very slowly. She looked at her aunt over the rim of her cup, but neither of them said anything. As she rose to leave, Mollie asked quickly, "Aunt Pat, what do you think the family would do if I dated some wild boys?"

Her aunt laughed and turned off the light. "Go to sleep. We'll save that for another day."

Chapter Thirteen

Mollie woke slowly, amid the hockey poster, small maple desks, and confining narrowness of her cousin Mark's bed. Gradually the memory of the night before grew up around her. She licked her teeth as she tried to retaste the cocoa, and rubbed her cheek against the softness of the flannel nightgown which was sticking to her neck, damp in the morning sunshine. Her eyes were stiff and crusty; perhaps she had been crying while she slept. Mollie allowed these thoughts to seep slowly into her consciousness, but her mind leapt back from the thought of Grandmother. She rubbed her sore eyes and felt the nameless terror suffuse her body again. Soon there would never again be Grandmother. Mollie shivered, closed her eyes against the overpowering light that had always prevented her when she had been at camp from looking into the sky to locate the ball. Without Grandmother she didn't have the flimsiest chance of success.

Reed will be here, she reminded herself. I shall be living with Reed. She drifted along on a stream of pleasant images; coming home from school and telling Reed about her day; going to movies with him; watching television together; reading poetry out loud just as they had done since she was a small girl.

Not quite the same, she thought, because now I'll be learning my rules, getting some practice, as Aunt Pat had phrased it. Mollie heard distant laughter in her head as she envisioned Reed's reaction to her visiting a strange boy's loft. A faint voice formed words, "If you stay there, you'll have to lie to him." Just keeping things private, Mollie consoled herself. There was no need to tell Reed every detail of what she was doing. Even Aunt Pat had said so. But Mollie would have to pretend to be going to one place and actually go to another. That was outright lying, and she had always prided herself on being honest. How dreadful to have to begin lying to Reed.

Mollie thought back to Hilary and that morning. Hilary had not been covering her actions; she had not lied to Mollie; Mollie had wanted her to. Rather than know the truth, she had tried to believe any of a number of possibilities. Hilary was her best friend and she couldn't accept the truth from her. Mollie fell back against the pillows. If Reed should happen to unearth some detail, something I consider "private"—she shook her head, hoping to elude the confusion that was growing by the minute. Maybe she should go for a walk. Some activity to clear her head of this muddle.

Slowly, like an invalid, she sat on the edge of the bed and wiggled her toes. She walked to the door, her neck bent under the weight of her head. The day had not begun in the apartment; the heavy drapes turned the living room gray; all the bedroom doors remained closed. Clara was not yet in the kitchen. What time was it?

Mollie looked around the room, but saw no clock. The boys still depended on adults to dole out their time—"Time to get up, time to do your homework, don't be late." She had to get outside, away from this loneliness hanging over her like stagnant air. At least there would be people on the street. And she could occupy her mind so she wouldn't have these unsettling thoughts.

She walked downtown, forcing herself to concentrate on shop windows, people's clothes, how many black dogs were passing her in the opposite direction. Anything to keep away from the danger area.

Mollie tried to insert herself into the early-morningness of the New York streets. She gathered in every passing face; reacted to each pair of wrinkled stockings, each seersucker jacket. For whom was the morning just the inevitability of a job? Which of them was going to the corner bakery for a fresh roll to liven up a solitary breakfast? She walked hurriedly so that they would all know she had a place where people were waiting for her. She was not alone.

But inside all this clutter, wavering just in front of her eyes, was Jaimie, shadowing the sun-dappled trees, blocking out the little black dogs, erasing the red leather leashes. Jaimie. She could feel the tips of his hair brushing her face. How could Aunt Pat think Mollie would want to keep him secret' She would burst if she didn't tell someone about him. She stopped in front of the seal pond and remembered Jaimie elbowing past the little kids. She watched the seals, their shapeless bodies like huge stuffed socks lying in the sun, and thought how Jaimie would laugh to see the old seal resting his whiskered snout on another seal's sleek neck. As she watched them lounging in the sun, Mollie felt as though she were seeing them with two pairs of eyes: hers and Jaimie's. She didn't need to tell Holly or Hilary about him. For the moment, knowing deep inside herself how he would enjoy the seals was enough.

Abruptly she walked away from the seals. Even warm feelings about Jaimie had to be ignored. Jaimie was gone from her life. Crossing to the zebras and lions Mollie wondered if she would ever possibly, on just the slimmest of chances, see Jaimie again. She paused to watch the men in cement-colored uniforms cleaning the cages.

"Take that camel inside while I get his cage," one of the attendants shouted. Mollie watched until they had pushed and prodded the camel inside the building, one leading from the front, one shoving from the back.

"How do you know the camel doesn't like water?" Mollie shouted to the attendant who was shooting arching geysers of water from a mammoth hose all around the cage.

"Camels don't like water," he answered, aiming the hose toward the cage corner nearest Mollie.

She backed away and smiled. Why doesn't he let the camel try it, just once, she thought resentfully. Her stomach tightened and she thought, "If I don't tell them about Jaimie, I'll have to decide myself. Nobody will lead me away."

She repeated this refrain until she realized she was standing in front of the bear cave.

She pulled herself onto a low smooth-surfaced rock, holding out her arms to protect herself from falling. This is

145

silly. I could barely reach the top with Jaimie holding on to me. But she slid her right foot out across the crevice to the next rock and swung her body across it, half-crouching, half-crawling. If I stay close to the rocks, I won't fall. At least I won't fall far. She got her whole body safely balanced on that rock, and continued, concentrating on the piece of rock directly in front of her, knowing that if she looked back or looked ahead, she would be too frightened by the overwhelming shape of each boulder to continue. It was slow, but she had lost all sense of time, of speed.

I think this is the rock we rested on. She rubbed her palm across the pebbly-rough granite, then harder and harder. She examined her hand, watched it turn red. Finally there was a cause for the ache she had been feeling since she had wakened that morning.

Crawling across this last rock to the cage bars, she scraped her knees, dragging them over the pitted stone. Her eyes were fixed on the iron bars; at last her hands closed over them, soothed by their smooth coldness. Jaimie's voice filled her head, stronger here, making her heart beat faster as she stared at her bruised gritty knees. "You have to make something yourself, for it to become your own."

Nothing belongs only to me, she thought. She shook the bars and moaned. The sound of her own voice seemed foreign in her ears. "All I have is family hand-me-downs. I've got to learn to weave my own cloth. I've got to start now." She was crying again. "Not with Reed." She shook the bars harder, banged her foot against the uncompromising rock. "I want to stay with Reed. I don't want to go to Springfield alone. I don't know how. I don't know how." She pressed her tear-hot face against her throbbing knees.

"It's time now," the inside voice said.

"Not yet," she answered.

"Now."

"After I live with Reed," she sobbed.

"You'll just keep asking him." Mollie clenched her teeth. "Get on with it; it's time to decide." The voice would not cease.

"No, no, no." She squeezed the cold bars, unrelenting against her powerless hands. "No," she screamed, her shout changing to a wail.

Gradually her moans grew softer because she knew that she could not shout louder than this persistent voice in her head. It was a new sound—the loudest Mollie had ever heard.